SPAIN'S
GREAT
UNTRANSLATED

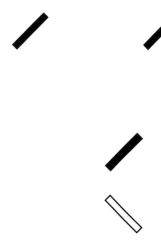

Spain's Great Untranslated

A Words without Borders Anthology

Edited by Javier APARICIO,
Aurelio MAJOR & Mercedes MONMANY

(WORDS *without* BORDERS)

This anthology is part of the SPAIN arts & culture
program and was made possible thanks to a charitable
contribution from the Spain-USA Foundation

SPAIN
arts &
culture

SPAIN/USA /
/ Foundation /

ISBN 978-0-9889051-0-8

Printed in the United States of America
Design by Toormix

Words without Borders
P.O. Box 1658
New York, NY 10276
www.wordswithoutborders.org

Photography Credits:
Cristina Fernández Cubas: © Pilar Aymerich
Pere Gimferrer: © Jorge de Cominges
Valerie Miles: © Nina Subin
Ignacio Martínez Pisón: © Nina Subin
Pedro Zarraluki: © Nina Subin
Olvido García Valdés: © Su Alonso & Inés Marful
Miquel de Palol: © L.M. Palomares

Acknowledgments

Words without Borders thanks The Spain-USA Foundation for its generous support of this project; Javier Aparicio, Aurelio Major, and Mercedes Monmany for their excellent work in selecting the authors and pieces to be included; and the authors and translators represented here.

Contents

$$\text{Fa} \xrightarrow[by]{trsltd} \text{Vm}$$

Mangled Flesh

Fernando ARAMBURU
Translated by Valerie MILES

HIS FATHER says, Son, if you see me crying when we go inside don't be afraid, you keep moving forward, they're my own things and they have nothing to do with you, coming here breaks my heart, but today I'm making good on something I've been promising you for a long time, Borja, I'm not putting it off any longer. Another March, noon, they said it's going to rain. We don't have to go inside if you don't want to, Dad, what you told me already and just seeing the station from the outside is enough. Red benches, the roof held in place by columns, the clock fixed to one of them. The platform looks as though it has been refurbished. A train headed for Alcalá comes in. People get off, people get on. A woman holds a small dog in her arms. The dog is wearing some kind of sweater. A kid with earphones slides into one of the cars as the doors are closing. Everyone is alive, no doubt about it, they're walking, breathing, all those things. The train takes off. The train speeds up. The train disappears into the distance. Electric cables overhead, the shine of the rails, clouds. By then the father, I can't explain what I'm feeling coming back to this place, and the son are alone on the platform. A pigeon pokes around for crumbs to eat, bobbing its head forward and backward as pigeons do. That's where it happened. The years have passed by like trains. One, then another, another. The boy directs his gaze to the spot where his father's empty sleeve is pointing. See that red trash can? The pigeon comes and goes beside it. I was thrown somewhere more or less around there, though I don't remember the trash can, and don't ask me how I got out of the train because I have no idea, maybe I flew. I felt something really hot on my face as I dragged myself along the ground. It smelled a lot like burned flesh, the heat moved over to my shoulder and then imagine, it started moving downward, I thought it was in my chest but it must have been my arm, and when it seemed to have reached my gut I said to myself you're fucked, Ramón, with a hole like that you're done for. The silence and the clouds of smoke, the silence of ruptured eardrums, and at last the people coming to our aid and the people running away on their good legs, with their good eyes and their whole bodies, how fortunate, though some of them were bleeding from their noses. It wasn't yet eight o´clock in the morning. I raised my head a little like this to see where that heat had gone now that it was turning into a tingling sensation that was growing ever more intense and I couldn't see any hole, what I did see halfway down my forearm was nothing but shreds of cloth soaked in blood, and I thought of your mother at home and of you too, you were so little, I had left you in your crib, asleep, and how was I going to hug you now if I didn't have a hand.

A HAND was the only thing poking out from underneath the blanket. A well-made hand with the nails painted red and a green trinket of a ring around her finger. The girl was still moving when they laid her on the ground. The Romanian man hardly paid attention to her. He had enough to deal with on his own. He had followed the policeman's instructions, going on foot with other wounded people to Daoiz y Velarde Sport Center. They asked if he understood Spanish. He answered yes and they told him to go stand by the wall and not to move from there, they would attend to him as soon as possible, do you understand? His legs were bare, skinned raw; he had lost his shoes and was trying to contain the blood gushing from his head with a cloth held tightly against the wound. A few minutes later, two healthcare workers laid the girl about two meters away from him. Her hair hid her face. At first the girl was moving. Her legs. Her back. Just a little bit. A slight tremor. Less and less. Then she stopped. They came to help her. Carefully, they turned her over. Nothing could be done. She was covered with a blanket a little later, leaving one of her hands exposed. A thin hand, pretty, now forever unmoving. The health workers continued on to the next body. The Romanian's eyelids were closing as he leaned against the wall. He fought to keep them open. They kept closing. They . . . Kep clo . . . K . . . Cl . . . The sudden flare of a cell phone roused him. The Romanian looked around till he found the happy tune some two meters away, under the blanket. He hesitated a moment. The high-pitched, frolicking notes didn't stop. They weren't coming from his phone. He had already been in touch with his family about what happened. The melody persisted with pleading insistence amid the chaos of health workers and gravely wounded bodies. He moved over to the blanket, picked up the edge, there was the phone, hanging halfway out the pocket of her charred coat. An older woman's voice on the other end began uttering words in a language the Romanian didn't understand. Maybe Polish or Russian. He realized he wasn't able to make himself understood. The voice grew alarmed and repeated what sounded like a name, the name of the body lying on the ground. Bombs on train. Bombs, lady. Boom. You understand? The Romanian pressed the button to hang up and returned to the place assigned to him by the health workers, next to the wall. Seconds later the girl under the blanket's phone rang again. The Romanian didn't move. He had enough with his own issues. The happy jingle continued, sounding for a long time from under the blanket.

THE BLANKET, why hadn't he thought of it before? He should have grabbed the blanket he kept in the trunk of his car. But they hadn't given him any time, goddammit, what a great way to start a new shift. A National Policeman had stopped him on Avenida Entrevías. What a God-awful mess. Like a scene from a war zone. Nothing had been announced on the radio yet. He hadn't heard the explosions but saw the smoke and the people dripping in blood, excuse the graphics, trying to catch the No. 24 bus. It must have been five or ten to eight. I'll never forget it. He hadn't meant to gawk, but the wounded who were huddled under the shelter of the bus stop, those ones, by God, those ones he had seen all right. Hold on there, kid, don't die on me, fuck, not here, just hold on, we're almost there. They had opened his cab door and pushed him in, hurry up now, closed the door and left him alone with the poor kid, eighteen, twenty years old, laid out there in the back seat, and the policeman said straight to the hospital, Sir. He took off for the 12th of October Clinic. The first ambulances passed by going the opposite direction. For lack of a handkerchief, since his wife didn't like them, they aren't hygienic she said and still says, Kleenex is better, it's disposable, that way you aren't hauling the boogers around in your pocket, you brute, you men are such brutes, he hung a dust rag out the window, and off he goes honking away so others yield the right of way and let him pass, no stoplights, no bullshit, and the municipal police, who must have already had news of the massacre, signaled him to go even faster. He wasn't able to see the wounded kid through the rearview mirror. Poor thing didn't say a word, not a complaint. Stay calm now, we'll be there in a jiffy, there are good doctors at 12th of October, my wife gave birth to a baby girl there, everything was perfect, clean, well-organized, so just be calm. It was a fib, his wife had given birth in Fuenlabrada Hospital, but what did it matter, all I meant to do was keep the poor kid's spirits up. The taxi started to smell of something burned. When my boss finds out about this . . . I would be grateful if you didn't vomit, that's for sure, but if it can't be avoided, better on the floor than on the seat, OK? I never stopped talking. Once in a while he would pick up strange clients. Surly types who didn't say a word the whole way. He's lived through a few tight spots, especially on the night shift, his wife would tell him he had better be careful, if they try to rob you, just give them everything, don't even think about resisting. But this was something else. Not a single complaint. Moribund. Maybe he was already gone when they loaded him into the cab. I stopped talking as soon as the red hospital building appeared in the distance. He hadn't stopped talking the whole way. The hospital staff took charge of the wounded kid, the dying kid, the dead kid who smelled of burned flesh, I didn't want to know. They asked him immediately to make room for other vehicles. Sirens could be heard getting closer and closer. He stopped as soon as he was able. The first thing he did was get his wife out of bed, put on the television, what should I do? Don't be a coward, call him up, I'm sure he'll understand. He dialed the number. I swear, I didn't have time to take the blanket out. There's a huge blood stain on the back seat. How huge, Vélez? Big enough that nobody can sit there, Boss, impossible. Calm down, Vélez. My wife says you should bring the car to our house, she'll treat the stain with some cleaning solution. Just calm down, I say. Listen, Sir, no, I'll pay for the cleaning out of my own pocket, even though it wasn't my fault. Don't make the problem worse for me, Vélez, just bring the taxi over here, today is going to be a difficult day for the city.

THE CITY, Saturday morning, seen from the inside of a car, appeared to have recovered a semblance of normalcy. Not a trace of the horrible event. I remember driving around Andalucía Avenue on the way to the southern mortuary, Dad at the wheel. A van driven by two boys stopped beside us at a red light. We could hear their music even though our windows were up. Mom said nowadays a lot of people have hearing problems before the age of thirty. I thought we've been left alone to our misfortune, after the deluge of news on the television, in the newspapers and such, people had gone back to their laughter and their private affairs. I guess that's just life. Even I'll forget my brother after a while, not entirely, at first I won't be able to get him out of my thoughts, then he'll start fading away, just like the commotion of those first hours has already faded from the conversations and memories of the people in Madrid. Grandpa insisted on coming with us. From the hallway he repeated what he had been saying over and over again since Thursday, loudly and clearly so that everyone could hear him from our respective bedrooms: I'll never forget, I'll never forgive and I am not going to cry. I won't give up a single tear to those bastards, I don't care if they're ETA, Al Qaeda, or whoever the hell they are. We were all too absorbed in our own sadness to answer him. At one point my dad gave him a pat on the shoulder as if to show that he sympathized and maybe also to insinuate that it was time to stop going on about it. At ten a.m. the entrance to the mortuary was packed. We parked following the orders of the municipal police. Then we checked the monitors in the vestibule looking for my brother's name, there it was, Mom was the first to see it, and the room where he was laid out. Dad stood in line behind other people dressed in mourning to ask how to get to that room there. Seven or eight people were helping at the counter so they quickly gave him instructions and he came over to us and whispered it's over there. A lot of hustle and bustle in the hallways. Reddened eyes, people hugging each other, the hum of conversations. A poster announced a free meal service in the basement for family and victims. We couldn't find my brother's room. Dad asked a couple of Red Cross volunteers. Very kindly, they brought us there. Meanwhile, Grandpa continued repeating in his typical curmudgeonly tone that he wasn't going to cry. Not a tear. He said so to the man and woman from the Red Cross: I will not cry. They responded that a team of psychologists was on call just upstairs. I don't cry, I have my pride, he told them. We saw an Ecuadoran flag on one of the doors and farther down, a Chilean one too. We recognized a lot of people from Latin American countries by their facial features. Also by the delicate and melodious way they have of pronouncing words. A priest came over to shake our hands. Grandpa was about to blurt out his sentence again, but Mom grabbed his arm to restrain him and whispered please. They offered to accompany us to the cemetery. We didn't want them to. Neither did we go to the basement. We weren't in the mood to fill our stomachs, although, to be honest, I did feel a pang of hunger and thirst. Back in the car, just out of the parking lot, I heard a strange noise at my side, a sort of moaning, a long sounding of the letter "u," *uuuu*, that at first I thought might have been one of us trying to imitate the sound of the wind in a scary movie, and when I looked behind me, I saw Grandpa's face afflicted and contorted in pain. He broke out crying disconsolately and in a trembling voice screamed murderers, murderers, cussing and saying he no longer believed in God. His sobs spread to all of us even though by now we were more serene and resigned than the first day. It got so bad that Dad had to pull the car over since he couldn't see the road through his tears. We couldn't speak for at least five minutes.

FIVE MINUTES before train 21431 arrived in Atocha station a girl dressed in a black parka and another in a green wool jacket happened to be there at the same time. It's a little past seven-thirty in the morning. Thursday. Both are on their way to work. The one in green freshens her lipstick, scrutinizing herself in a small mirror she's taken from her purse. The one in black hurries through the last few pages of a Pérez Reverte novel. The one who is reading lives in Getafe; the one who wears lipstick, in Parla. The one from Getafe has Andean features, the one from Parla, Mediterranean. They're part of the flood of students and workers who transfer between commuter trains in Atocha early in the morning. They're accustomed to seeing each other, but they never say hello. They take the train that comes from Alcalá de Henares to Alcobendas every working day. Then at the Nuevos Ministerios stop, one of them heads for the subway while the other goes up to the street, and they lose sight of each other until the next day, unless they happened to have gotten on different cars, in which case they would have lost sight of one another earlier on, in Atocha, if they had ever seen each other at all, which doesn't always happen. It's the eleventh day of March. It's chilly and gray, almost cold. As yet a normal day. Two kids run down the escalator as if they were afraid of missing the train that hadn't yet arrived. Maybe they're joking around and racing. An urban mouse scurries around a blackened ballast. The train from Alcalá conceals the busy mouse as it makes its entry into the station, stops at the usual track and opens its doors. People get off. People get on. The girl from Getafe has a finger stuck in the Pérez Reverte novel to keep the page she was reading. The one from Parla gets on behind her and sits down nearby. They don't speak. They've already exchanged glances once, so they don't do it again. As they await the *beep-beep-beep* announcing that the doors are closing, they are suddenly overwhelmed by a colossal explosion which jolts the car violently. The light goes out. The girl in green steps out of the train. To her right, almost at the end of the long string of cars, she sees billowing columns of smoke. The voice of a passenger behind her asks if there's been a collision. Seconds later, the girl in black steps onto the platform. Muted screams can be heard. Some silhouettes rushing around crouch beside bodies that are blown to pieces, scattered around the ground. The girl in black says Holy Mother of God as she pulls a cell phone out of her pocket. The one in green doesn't say a thing. Instead, she runs toward the escalator, where at that moment there are others on the way up who aren't in a rush. Just as she's about to reach the upper deck, she glances back at the platform. Smoke is still pouring out of one of the cars at the tail end. She can just make out in the distance what appears to be someone dragging themselves along the ground. In the midst of it all, she happens to come across the girl in black approaching the escalator below with her book in her hand. One is on the upper deck, the other on the lower deck, their eyes meet for less than a second before a huge explosion behind the girl in black launches a blast of flames against the platform and a dense cloud of swirling smoke and splinters engulfs a large number of people. The girl in green has just enough time to verify that the girl in black is about to reach the bottom of the escalator. Hardly has she turned around to continue making her way to the exit when she hears another explosion, this time very nearby. Dazed, she falls to the ground. A young man coming from behind falls on top of her before a cloud of smoke and dust overtakes them both. Coughing, eyes irritated, she makes it to the street and walks around as if she was lost. She walks up Paseo del Prado not daring to look back, and stops a taxi. In the office, everyone already knows what's going on. Her colleagues see how listless she is. They ask her boss to let her go home. The boss accedes. But she says she isn't leaving, she's afraid to leave, she has work to get done. A colleague drives her home to Parla later in the morning. Days come, days go, one afternoon she comes across the photos of the victims on the Internet. She studies the rows of faces looking for the Andean features of the girl she used to see on the train in the mornings. Curious, she wonders what her name was. Yet despite carefully perusing the nearly two hundred photos, she can't locate her. She views numerous female faces. Women of a certain age, young women, adolescents. But the photo of the woman she's looking for isn't there. She's relieved. Her boyfriend comes in. He asks what she's doing. She answers I could have been with these poor people. Her face reveals sadness. Why do you say that? I could have helped, but instead I left. Her boyfriend consoles her. For the next few weeks she takes a different route to work. It's a more complicated way, but it allows her to avoid confronting the place of her nightmares. She holds out through the end of March, but how to avoid it, she goes back to her usual morning routine, changing trains in Atocha station. One day in early summer, a little after seven-thirty in the morning, she awaits the train for Alcala, engrossed in watching a little mouse running along the tracks. Suddenly and for no reason she turns her head and sees her again, dressed in light clothing, it was a hot day after all. A little closer now, she glimpses a scar running from ear to neck forming a noticeable, rose-colored swirl around her cheek. The girl from Getafe walks straight up to her. She stops about a half-meter away. They look at each other for a few seconds, both very serious. Suddenly, without saying a word, they lock in an embrace in the center of the platform. A hug they repeat every morning.

EVERY MORNING Lorenzo carries out the same ritual when he wakes up. He looks over from his bed at the square of sky visible through his window and says today is a new day for me and I'm going to enjoy it. He whispers both sentences as if they were a childhood prayer. He hasn't skipped a day in the past four months, Monday through Sunday. It started a few days after the morning some men tried to kill him and others saved him. Thanks to the latter he feels reconciled with life: also, somehow, with human beings. With one of them in particular who's been in his thoughts every waking hour. He tried to locate him for weeks following his release from the hospital, trying to find out who he is, to be able to thank him, to embrace him and see if he could ever repay the huge favor he had done him in saving his life. Yesterday, he finally had the enormous pleasure of receiving his phone call and they arranged to meet up in a modest tavern on Albufera Avenue. Lorenzo had placed a number of advertisements in the newspaper, paying for them out of his own pocket. In them, he succinctly explained his case. Obsessed over trying to find the man, it took him weeks to finally fulfill his wish. He had appeared on a Telemadrid program, to no avail. Finally, he had been invited to a radio show where he explained his experience as a victim of the attack yet another time and gave his phone number, enunciating the digits carefully so he would be understood correctly. His tenacity (stubbornness, according to his mother) paid off. Lorenzo's case is similar to those of many others. Given the circumstances, Son, you were very lucky. Lorenzo doesn't like the word lucky, though he realizes that his mother does have a point and so he doesn't contradict her. He was riding the train that's now known as the Tellez Street train. He dislikes the designation. Trains don't go down streets. His mother lets him voice his opinion or else she says Son, you were less contentious before. I'm not being contentious, and then he reiterates his intention of never looking back, of accepting life as it is and enjoying it if it allows. That's much better, Lorenzo, but try not to forget it in five minutes. He was lying among the rubble of the train, aware that he was bleeding to death, unable to get up.

That's when the man appeared from out of the smoke, his clothes in shreds. He spoke broken Spanish and it was hard to understand him. Others ran, but he stayed, and pulled the shirt from his body and tied it around Lorenzo's thigh, a little above his knee. That was the last Lorenzo knew before gaining consciousness again the next day in a hospital bed at Gregorio Maranon. A doctor told him that without the tourniquet they would have had to amputate his leg and another told him that whoever had applied first aid had saved his life. He returned from the tavern on Albufera Avenue smiling. It wasn't him, he said to his mother. What do you mean it wasn't him? This one's a young Polish man who speaks passable Spanish, who was in the train and helped a number of wounded passengers. One of his neighbors told him that I was looking for him, and gave him our phone number so he could call and we met up, but he isn't the person who helped me, that person is a little older than him. So what did you do? What could I do? I hugged him so hard I nearly broke his ribs. And the chocolates? I hope he likes them. You said good-bye and that's it? His name is Ludoslaw, he had to write it out on a napkin, he's been in Spain for eight months, he doesn't remember how many people he helped before the emergency workers came, and tomorrow morning I'm going to call Ruano. I want him to help with the visa documents for two of his sons who still live in Poland. Did you tell him the truth? What truth? What truth do you think I mean, that he isn't the person who helped you. I preferred to make a friend. After all, who can say that it's not me who's mistaken. Maybe I am.

I AM not sure there's a way that we can fix that man. He's not the same as before and he isn't going to change. The priest came over to try and convince him that God exists. He shook his head in denial without letting go of the shotgun, right there, in the kitchen. Of course He exists, even now at this time He's inside of you. Well he better come on out of there so I can fill him with holes like he deserves. Holy Mother of God, how can anyone talk like that to a priest? Later he went out to shoot in the corral, like he's been doing every afternoon since we got back from Madrid. The neighbors sympathize with him. The first day they called the Civil Guard, but now there's no reason for it. He's being consumed by a white rage. But I know, because I sleep with him, that he cries under the sheets at night. He sort of twitches a little in the darkness. That's when I know he's crying and I don't say anything. We don't speak about that Thursday the 11th. My sister-in-law came over one day and the three of us stayed at home without opening our lips. She's aware of the favor she owes us. Because it was my husband and I who went to Pavilion 6 of the Convention Center in Madrid to identify what was left of my nephew inside a body bag. Her brother told her You're not going there. But it's my son. Yes he is, but you're not going. On our way to Madrid we were worried that something bad could have happened, but not the worst, not that. The boy was hurt, sure, since every morning in Guadalajara he would get on one of the trains that blew up. My sister-in-law didn't stop calling his cell phone and he never picked up. At first she called constantly, one call following the next, then every half hour. There was no trace of the boy. So the three of us took off for Madrid in our car and we spent the day going from one hospital to another. None of them could tell us anything. They sent us here, they sent us there. Around eight in the evening we found out that they had been taking cadavers to the Convention Center for identification. We told my sister-in-law, whose nerves were already shot, You aren't coming, if God has taken him we'll let you know but it's better you don't see him because it's going to be tough. And when I say tough, my husband told her, I know what I'm talking about, go home now, for Christ's sake, don't make me say things twice. We went together, him and me, since I'm like his shadow. We were waiting over two hours. My hands shook. They let us go ahead of others since we came in from outside the city. We were left alone with some psychologists. I mean, we couldn't go in just like that where the dead were, that's something I can understand, we had to prepare ourselves. Those poor psychologists. Every time I think back . . . One of them was very young, his eyes were red. Go ahead and cry, don't hold it back, I told him, anyway, one tear more or one tear less isn't going to change anything. My husband didn't stop asking if the boy's name and surname was on any one of the victim lists. Distraught, so distraught though without screaming like we heard others scream when we got there. They explained what we were going to see, that it wasn't going to be pleasant and all that, and to make matters worse my nephew didn't have identification, I don't know, he must have lost his ID in the explosion, so there wasn't anything we could do but have a look at some photographs, how gruesome, if you recognize him let us know, mangled flesh, mangled flesh, more mangled flesh and more, me praying to myself and feeling like asking for copies of all the photos to send them to the mothers of the people who had done all of that. Eventually, that could be him, I said, are you sure, my nephew wore a ring in his ear like that, yeah that's right, Christ, my husband laughed at him about a month ago are you a faggot or what, but he loved him so much, he was more than a nephew to us, he was like the son that God hadn't given to us. It was unfortunate, had they been able to identify him by his ID card we might have been spared from looking in the bag. We still had a long wait. I guess the stricken weren't supposed to see each other. So as not to deepen the grief or something like that. And there he was packaged like a heap of misery, with a tag where CT and a number were written, a bag with a few belongings, and yes, it was him, at least the head was his, the rest who could possibly say. We walked out in silence, others sobbed, we didn't. We went back to the village and my husband hasn't been the same ever since then. At times he just stares blankly at nothing for a long time, without blinking, and it scares even me. Every afternoon he goes out to the corral with a shotgun, a shot here, a shot there. Yesterday I came across the shotgun leaning against the wall in the hallway so I picked it up and I don't know what I was thinking, maybe I wanted to imagine what he was feeling, I made my way through the hens and shot a round against the garden wall. In the kitchen he asked me how many I had killed. I stood there looking at him and it came to me. Got two of them, I said, keeping up with the gag. Along with the three I killed myself that makes five, not bad at all for today.

TODAY he arrived at the station more tired than usual. He had stayed up late last night watching television. He was curious to know who would win *The Jungle of the Famous*, a program he abhorred, but if he didn't watch it he would be left out of the conversations with his colleagues at work. The bullfighter won, goddamnit, instead of the water polo player who he preferred. Then he listened to the commentaries on the Madrid–Bayern Munich match. They hadn't played well, Roberto Carlos's absence was evident, Zidane made the winning goal, his eyelids closed and he went to bed for the last time in his life. But how could he have known that. He bought a copy of *Marca* at the usual time in Alcala station. He checked his watch. There's still time for his first cigarette of the day. He had better enjoy it because there won't be another. An acquaintance greets him. Hey, you said you were quitting! The last one, he answers sarcastically, unaware of the fact that it's the truth. And he goes on reading the sports newspaper in the third car of train 21435. Some days he gets on the first car, or the fifth, upstairs or downstairs, it doesn't really matter, but today he made the worst choice of his life. Along some stretches the tracks aren't laid straight and so the passengers' heads sway softly. There are familiar faces, a lot of Latin Americans and students. He folds his copy of *Marca* intending to read it on his way home, he sure would like that, he doesn't know what's in store for him, where? He'll know soon enough. He sets the newspaper on his lap as he leans back to catch a little snooze. A quick glance out the window before his eyelids close gives the impression that it's the landscape that is going by at full speed while the train is standing still. He meets the smile of the girl sitting next to him. Can I? She points her finger at his masculine attributes. Amusing mistake. She means the newspaper. Sure, go ahead. He leans back, eager to please her like a man smitten by feminine beauty, to the point of trying to imitate her smile, though his teeth aren't as white nor his lips as plump. Just before Vicalvaro, a young man with black curls who is sitting a few seats away gets up and stands in front of the door. The train comes to a halt with the usual squeaking, or maybe not, what does it matter. People get off, people get on. More people get on than off. The same thing happens after a while at the Santa Eugenia stop. If they knew what is about to happen in a few minutes, at 7:38, in El Pozo, they would all jump off and run. But it's already too late, the doors have closed, the landscape has already begun moving again and the passengers let their heads bob in the usual way, stimulating a collective drowsiness at the tender hour of sunrise. Those who just got off in Vilcalvaro or in Santa Eugenia will lay themselves to rest at night in their warm beds and in the morning, which will be rainy, they'll be able to leave their homes complaining about how bad the weather is. Only a few of those who are still in the third car of train 21435 will see the clouds. Speaking of Vicalvaro, the girl who had asked him for his *Marca* suddenly says oh dear, that young man forgot his backpack, she points to it under the seat that is now occupied by another lady, oh yeah, you're right. With her twenty-something woman's hand she taps lightly on the glass to get the attention of the boy with the black curls, down on the platform, who turns around with a quick feline movement of his neck, as if expecting the call, his black, penetrating eyes, his gripped or worried eyebrows, who knows what he would be thinking. He looks the other way immediately, moving toward the platform's exit close behind another boy who has made some sort of urgent signal with his head. The poor kid left without his backpack, what a shame, she says. How scatterbrained, he adds, how can anyone forget a bag that size. Well, we're all half-asleep at this time of the morning, she tries to justify the stranger, when the ticket collector comes we'll let him know about it, they'll get it back to him. If some shyster doesn't get it beforehand he responds, it's not like the world is at a loss for bad people.

PEOPLE fallen on the tracks. People who exited a train stopped near ours and hurried over to help us. People who lived in the surrounding areas, with bottles of water, rags (or towels, I don't know), and utensils from a first-aid kit. People who threw blankets from their windows. People who called the police on their cell phones, the civil protection associations, the fire department. This is the first image that comes to mind of the minutes after the explosion. The people I glimpsed when I could raise my head a little, using all my strength. People as unfortunate as me, and even more than me, when all is said and done I'm alive and able to tell the tale, and there was that other person who came to our aid out of compassion, solidarity, and goodwill. The explosion had sent me flying through the air. I fell next to the tracks. I couldn't get up. When I began to realize what had happened I couldn't feel a thing, honestly, no pain. I went so far as to think you're dead, don't get your hopes up, you're observing it all from the other side. I didn't doubt for a second that we were the victims of a terror attack. I touched my face and also my teeth and I grabbed a stone to see if I still belonged to reality. I remember saying in my mind don't worry, Mother, I'm alive. I had lost a shoe and a sock. There were only a few shreds left of my pants. My legs were exposed, covered in wounds, as if they had been shot with an automatic weapon, and there was a gash on my knee where the tip of a bone stuck out. My head was bleeding heavily. I didn't notice my broken ankle until they told me about it at the Daoiz and Velarde Sport Center where I was given first aid before being put in an ambulance. And then all those poor people scattered around the ground. And the weeping. And the cries for help that got weaker and weaker. And those who didn't move. Dead. Maybe. Surely. That woman lying next to me. She whispered in a pitiful voice help me, help me, which is how I realized I couldn't get up. I was able to drag myself about a half a meter closer to her by leaning on my elbows. I was close enough to grab her hand. A slight, warm hand. I saw people running away suddenly and thank goodness because another detonation broke through the air. I couldn't move. I had the feeling that I had melted into the earth from the waist down. I couldn't see the woman anymore. Help me. My blood filled my eyes. For a while I could hear her sobs, her pleas, feel her hand in my fingers. Every once in a while I squeezed a little. She did the same thing. It was a way of communicating though we never said a word except to confirm to each other that we were still there, that we hadn't perished. It was difficult for me to speak to her, dryness had taken over my mouth and it felt as though my throat were full of hot sand. She didn't answer. I squeezed her hand. She didn't react. I squeezed again. I could tell she didn't have strength left. It was harder and harder for me to maintain my posture. Suddenly I felt a pain in my chest that made it extremely difficult to breathe. I think I was swallowing my own blood. I separated my fingers. The woman's hand slipped away. I tried to hold on to it. I couldn't.

I COULDN'T go downstairs, I'm so sorry, I recalled the accident, I had just about opened the front door but I just couldn't do it. The first explosion woke him up. The shock wave shattered the glass of his bedroom windows. Be careful when you stand up Salome said, don't walk around barefoot. What was that? Another explosion went off in the street below and the house trembled, and then another and it trembled again. I think something tragic is going on down there, she said, already dressed to run off to the newsroom at the paper where she works, but I don't want to look myself, can you come over here please? They looked out the kitchen window, he in pajamas and slippers, and she, a journalist to the core, holding a camera. She took a number of photos of the train stopped on the tracks closest to the street. The shattered cars revived in him the memory of the images of his traffic accident in January, the twisted steel, the feeling of impotence, the blood and all that, why go into it any further. Obviously that was an accident and this was intentional. People vacated the train, some through the windows. They wandered around, blood and screams, among fallen bodies, not a few of them unmoving, and regardless there were those who stopped and crouched over to hold the head of someone gravely wounded. Others ran or walked aimlessly, wobbly-legged, scared, stunned. Salome held on to his arm and he said, just to say something, to not stay silent, because the sound of the sirens was making him nervous, we'll have to sweep up the glass. He made out the figure of a man with a bloody face, lying on the ground in the swath of land that separated the train tracks from the houses. He recoiled a step as if pushed back violently by the memory of his father lying on that frozen road in Segovia. Neighbors' voices could be heard from windows of the building on the floor above and the floors below, offering help and exchanging short, quick sentences with the survivors. The first one out, a boy who lived on the ground floor on the right hand side, crossed below the fence where there was a hole. He ran holding a stack of blankets in his arms. The people who live on the second floor came behind him with bottles of water and a first-aid kit. In the meantime, they rang the doorbell. He heard Salome from the kitchen talking with someone who seemed very upset. He overheard their conversation from the kitchen, though now he stood away from the window, there was a background of confused voices and hurried steps in the building's stairway. Get dressed, we need to help those poor people. They arranged to bring blankets to keep the wounded people warm, and the first-aid kit, and don't forget the cell phone because some people won't have one or will have lost them and grab whatever else you think will be useful, sweetheart, I'm taking off, I'll wait for you downstairs, hurry up. He couldn't. He did get dressed quickly. But he just couldn't. I'm a coward. He walked into the bathroom. What's Salome going to say? What kind of a man is she with? Have you no heart? He caught sight of his face in the mirror and broke into tears. He shook violently and felt a sharp pang of anxiety overwhelm him slowly but surely, finally taking his breath away. He stopped just in front of the door, panicked, his heart pounding. He reached the doorknob with his hand but he wasn't able to turn it. He squeezed it for a long time. The ambulance and fire truck sirens resounded throughout the house. He stood fixed in place, staring at the furry back of his hand as if he had never seen it before, that was already transmitting heat to the doorknob. Suddenly, he saw once again the sheets of ice covering the asphalt, the curve that he took too quickly, his father had warned him, be careful Guzman, it was the last thing he said. He would have liked to erase the memory, to expel it from his thoughts like someone who vomits a toxic substance, but he couldn't, he simply couldn't, and once again the scene that had been torturing him for two months ran through complete in his head: the truck, the broken glass, the insupportable certainty that the man lying at the side of the road, covered by a blanket, was his father.

Pg $\xrightarrow[by]{trsltd}$ Wb

from "Rhapsody"

Pere GIMFERRER
Translated by Willis BARNSTONE

XV

The time has come to say good-bye;
with farewells comes wind to the vineyard
like dark Valpolicella wine
in the hand of dark winter dyes:
parks, far stations pass by
winter platforms, by hills
that lose their color on being dyed
into crystals by thinking light;
so we head for the center, not to flight
or the abyss but the carnation of time,
of what spots us in the flaming mirror.
So clouds in their service pass by
like the Holy Procession of Phantoms
like the Pilgrimage of the Rose Bush;
not Monsalvat, not Camelot or Tripoli
but the Holy Grail of our dreams.
And in all one's life this handful,
this clump of carnations remains;
so many words only to say
this silver pilgrim cloak of love.

XV

El tiempo nuestro es ya de despedida:
con los adioses viene el viento al pámpano,
como en Valpolicella oscurecida
en la mano de tinte del invierno:
parques, lejanas estaciones pasan
por andenes de invierno, por los cerros
que pierden su color al ser tiznados
en los cristales por la luz que piensa:
así vamos al centro, no a la huida
o a lo abismal, sino al clavel del tiempo,
que nos ve en un espejo llameante,
en un planeta de agua incandescente.
Así las nubes en su oficio pasan,
como Santa Compaña o estantigua,
como la romería del rosal:
no Monsalvat, no Camelot ni Trípoli,
sino el santo Grial de nuestros sueños.
Y, de toda la vida, este puñado,
esta gavilla de claveles queda:
tanta palabra por decir tan sólo
la esclavina de plata del amor.

XVI

The evening hour glows
and waters on the walkway darken,
we are zigzagging on the road
like the plot unravels in Buñuel
when the wrong way contradicts
the sacred official quadrille:
so the always serpentine poem
is at the end pure magnetism
with clarity of an abandoned hotel
off season, with blind eyes
more lively its balcony fever
in the frontispiece of escritoires
that visit the fingers of the moon,
the keystrokes of lunar wind,
in Magritte's night of accessories.
We liked it all, but in the end
we had it all; having lived
is the sweetest taste of the cherry
and seasoning of a broken night.
Bowing, the past's watery mass
gazes at the shooting star of day,
a cannonade of weird obscurity,
the cannonade of dying love.

XVI

Es charolada la hora nocturna
y son oscuras las aguas del paso.
Por el camino vamos en zigzag,
como en el desenlace de Buñuel,
cuando el rumbo aberrante contradice
la contradanza del oficio sacro:
así el poema, siempre en serpenteo,
pero al fin todo pura imantación:
con claridad de hotel abandonado
fuera de temporada, de ojos ciegos,
mas vivos en su fiebre de balcones,
en las escribanías de fachada
que visitan los dedos de la luna,
el teclear del aire selenita,
en la noche de atrezzo de Magritte.
Lo queríamos todo, pero, al cabo,
lo hemos tenido todo: haber vivido
es el sabor dulzón de la ciruela
y el condimento de la noche rota.
Agachadas, las gachas del pasado
miran pasar los bólidos del día:
un cañoneo en la tiniebla extraña,
el cañoneo del morir de amor.

XVII

In a box of air comes a flaming curtain,
the look of Jean-Michel Frank's art deco,
the headwaiter taster of light,
a flight of fallen dragonflies
in the slim drafts of daybreak,
in the garden hunting party
the magistrate on Ferrara's hillock
is confounded by the evening hour,
Boldini's sofa with nude woman
in black stockings, Casati design
and his hypnotic zoo of gold and glass.
We are yesterday's gardeners
but also the Argonauts
who captured the golden fleece
in the cenacle of darkened divination,
like the theater in Lady from Shanghai.
Everything alive goes with me,
with you goes what you lived,
but a handful of rose eyelids
on a night of frozen numb light
is what is lived by two, rug
for a Scheherazade arcoirisada rose
in a Baghdad with laced shoes of fire
like the Paris night when Proust
in night alarm saw Grosse Bertha
turbaned in a swallow-tail mask.
On the night of pendants and festoons
we carry our offering—our whole being.
Twilight falls through the turbine
of mute oxen and teaches us
the insistence of living what day holds,
the abandonment of living love;
face to face we watch each other in filmed night,
Day for Night, the mirror's impracticabilities,
because love is a mirroring,
is possession of body and its images,
image painters of possession,
possession of truth for both;
we are protagonists of resplendence.

XVII

En la caja del aire va el telón encendido,
la mirada art déco, Jean-Michel Frank;
viene el maestresala de la luz,
un vuelo de libélulas caídas
en los esbozos del amanecer:
por una cacería de jardines
el podestá en la loma de Ferrara
se desconcierta en la nocturnidad:
el sofá de Boldini, la Casati
y su hipnótico zoo de oro y rocalla:
somos los jardineros del ayer,
pero también somos los argonautas
(qui conquit la toison), en el cenáculo
de las agorerías vueltas sombra,
en las sombras chinescas del vivir,
como el teatro en Lady from Shangai.
Todo lo que vivía va conmigo,
contigo va lo que viviste tú,
pero un puño de párpados de rosa
en una noche de luz arrecida
es lo vivido por los dos, alfombra
para una Scherezade arcoirisada
en un Bagdad con borceguí de llamas
como la noche en París que vio Proust,
en alarmas nocturnas, Grosse Bertha,
turbantes en las máscaras de frac.
A cuestas en la noche de colgantes,
llevamos nuestra ofrenda: todo el ser.
Por la turbina de los bueyes mudos
el crepúsculo cae, y nos enseña,
en el desistimiento del vivir,
la insistencia en vivir que tiene el día,
lo indesistido del amor que vive:
cara a cara nos vemos en la noche filmada,
Day for Night, aporías del espejo,
porque el amor es un espejear,
la posesión del cuerpo en sus imágenes,
imagineros de la posesión,
la posesión de la verdad de ambos:
somos protagonistas del fulgor.

$$\textbf{Cfc} \xrightarrow[\textit{by}]{\textit{trsltd}} \textbf{Lg}$$

The Baghdad Clock

Cristina FERNÁNDEZ CUBAS
Translated by Lucy GREAVES

I never feared them nor did they ever do anything to frighten me. They were there, next to the stove, mixed up with the crackling of firewood, the taste of freshly baked bollos, the to-and-fro of the old women's skirts. I never feared them, perhaps because in my imagination they were pale and beautiful, listening as we did to the stories that took place in nameless hamlets, waiting for the right moment to let themselves be heard, to whisper to us wordlessly: "We're here, just like every night." Or to hide in the dense silence which announced: "Everything you're hearing is true. Tragically, painfully, sweetly true." It could happen at any moment. The sound of the waves after a storm, the passing of the last goods train, the trembling of crockery in the cupboard or the unmistakable voice of Olvido, immersed in her alchemy of pots, pans, and kettles:

"It's the spirits, girl, it's the spirits."

More than once, my eyes half-closed, I believed in them.

How old would Olvido have been back then? Whenever I asked her age the old woman shrugged her shoulders, looked at Matilde out of the corner of her eye, and remained impassive, shelling peas, darning socks, dividing lentils into little piles, or all of a sudden she would remember the urgent need to go down to the cellar for firewood and stoke the salamander stove on the top floor. One day I tried to get it out of Matilde. "As old as the world," she said, laughing.

Matilde's age, on the other hand, never stirred my curiosity. She too was old, she walked hunched over, her hair was gray, turned yellowish by eau de cologne, bound into a small bun, tight as a ball, out of which stuck needles and pins. She had a lame leg that could predict the weather and do other tricks besides, which, as the years went by, she couldn't recall as well as she would have liked. But next to Olvido, Matilde seemed younger, somewhat less wise and much less experienced, although her voice sounded sweet when she showed us the misty glass and made us believe that outside wasn't the sea nor the beach, nor the train tracks, nor even the Paseo, but steep and inaccessible mountains around which ran packs of furious, hungry wolves. We knew—Matilde had told us plenty of times—that no God-fearing person should, on nights like this, leave the warmth of his or her home. Because who else but a sinning soul, condemned to walk among us, would dare to face such darkness, such cold, such terrifying moans coming from the bowels of the Earth? Then it was Olvido's turn to speak. Slowly, surely, knowing that from then on she had us, that soon the light of the oil lamp would be concentrated on her face and her old woman's wrinkles would give way to the rosy complexion of a girl, to the fearsome face of a gravedigger tormented by his memories, to a visionary monk, perhaps to a miraculous nun . . . Until firm footsteps, or a light tapping of heels, announced the arrival of unwelcome guests. Or until they, our friends, made it known through Olvido that the time had come to rest, to eat our semolina soup or to turn out the light.

Yes, Matilde, as well as her soothsaying leg, possessed the gift of gentleness. But in that time of unwavering dedication I had taken Olvido's side, or perhaps Olvido had left me no other choice. "When you're older and you get married, I'll go to live with you." And I, nestled in my protector's lap, couldn't imagine what that third person willing to share our lives would be like, nor could I see any reason to leave my family or to abandon, some day, the house by the beach. But Olvido always decided for me. "The apartment will be small and sunny, with no stairs, cellar, or roof terrace." And I had no option but to imagine it just so, with a spacious kitchen where Olvido would potter as she liked, and a big wooden table with three chairs, three glasses, and three porcelain plates . . . Or rather, two. The presence of the stranger that Olvido's predictions attributed to me didn't fit in my new kitchen. "He'll eat later," I thought. And I moved his chair to a hypothetical dining room which my fantasy had absolutely no interest in depicting.

But on that hot December Sunday, when the children danced around the package that had arrived, I looked closely at Olvido's face and it seemed that there wasn't room for a single wrinkle more. She was strangely stiff, oblivious to requests for scissors and knives, isolated from the commotion that the unexpected gift had caused in the sitting room. "As old as the world," I remembered, and for a moment I was filled with the certainty that the chair I had so easily displaced to the dining room didn't belong to my blurry, supposed, future husband.

They had brought it that same morning, wrapped in thick brown paper, tied up with cord and rope like a prisoner. It looked like a humiliated giant, laid out as it was on the carpet, suffering the dancing and shrieking of the excited, restless children, all sure until the last moment that they alone would be the recipients of the oversized toy. My mother, acting like a spoiled cat, closely followed all attempts to reveal the mystery. A new wardrobe? A sculpture, a lamp? But no, woman, of course not. It was a work of art, a curiosity, a bargain. The antiques dealer must have lost his mind. Or perhaps it was old age, a mistake, other worries. Because the price was laughable for such a wonder. All we had to do was take off the last bits of sticking tape, the cellophane that protected the most fragile parts, open the little door and steady the pendulum. A grandfather clock almost three meters tall, gold-plated numerals and hands, a rudimentary yet perfect mechanism. We would have to clean it, prop it up, use polish to hide the inevitable ravages of time. Because it was a very old clock, dated 1700, from Baghdad, probably the work of Iraqi craftsmen for some European client or other. That was the only way to understand why the numeration was Arabic and the lower part of the body featured a relief carving of a festive group of people. Dancers? Guests at a banquet? The years had blurred their features, the pleats of their clothing, the delicacies that we could still make out on the worm-eaten surface of a table. But why didn't we decide right away to lift our eyes, to gaze at the clock face, to contemplate the set of scales which, transferring the weight of a few grains of sand, set the carillon in motion? And already the children, equipped with buckets and spades, had gone out onto the Paseo, looked right and left, crossed the road and rolled about on the beach which was no longer a beach but a far-off and dangerous desert. But it didn't need that much sand. No more than a handful, and above all a moment of silence. Crowning the face, covered in dust, was the day's final surprise, the most delicate collection of clockwork pieces we could have imagined. Tiny suns, planets and stars waiting for the first notes of a melody to set them in motion. In less than a week we would know all the mechanism's secrets.

They installed it on the landing halfway up the stairs, at the top of the first flight, a space that seemed to have been made to measure. You could admire it from the hall, from the first-floor landing, from the soft armchairs in the sitting room, from the trapdoor that led up onto the roof. When, after a few days, we got the right amount of sand and the carillon let out the notes of an unknown melody for the first time, the clock seemed to all of us to be taller and more beautiful. The Baghdad Clock was there. Arrogant, majestic, measuring with a dull tick-tock our every movement, our breathing, our childhood games. It was as if it had been there from time immemorial, as if it alone had occupied that space, perhaps it was the haughtiness of its stance, its security, the respect it inspired in us when, at nightfall, we left the peaceful kitchen to go up to our bedrooms on the top floor. Visitors were enchanted, and my father kept congratulating himself for the shrewdness and timing of his acquisition. A unique opportunity, a beauty, a work of art.

Olvido refused to clean it. She claimed vertigo, migraines, old age, and rheumatism. She alluded to sight problems, she who could find a grain of barley in a sack of wheat, the head of a pin in a heap of sand, the smallest stone in a handful of lentils. Clambering up a ladder wasn't a job for an old lady. Matilde was much younger and, what's more, she hadn't been at the house for nearly as long. Because she, Olvido, possessed the privilege of seniority. She had raised my father's siblings, been present at my birth and at that of my brothers, that freckly pair who never left Matilde's skirts. But she didn't have to make a point of her rights nor grab hold of my plaits so tightly. "Olvido, you're like one of the family." And hours later, in the solitude of my parents' bedroom: "Poor Olvido. Getting old is hard."

I don't know if the strange unease that would soon take hold of the house came all at once, as I remember it now, or if maybe that's the unavoidable distortion of memory. But what's for sure is that Olvido, some time before the shadow of fatality loomed over us, began to behave like a distrustful feline with her ears always pricked up, her hands twitching, attentive to every breeze, the slightest murmur, the creaking of doors, the passing of the goods train, the fast train, the express, the quotidian trembling of pans on the shelves. But now it wasn't the spirits who asked for prayers, nor sinning friars condemned to suffer on Earth for long years. Life in the kitchen had become filled with a tense and stifling silence. It was no use insisting. The hamlets, lost in the mountains, had become distant and inaccessible, and our attempts, when we came home from school, to get new stories out of her were left as unanswered questions, floating in the air, dancing about, dissipating along with smoke and sighs. Olvido seemed shut up inside herself, and although she pretended to work hard at scrubbing the pans, polishing the wardrobes and cupboards and bleaching the grout between the mosaic tiles, I knew she was crossing the dining room, cautiously going up the first few stairs, stopping at the landing and observing. I imagined her observing, with the courage granted her by being not entirely present, in front of the brass pendulum but still safe in her world of kettles and frying pans, a place where the beating of the clock didn't reach and where she could easily smother the sound of the inevitable melody.

But she hardly spoke. Only that now distant morning, when my father, crossing seas and deserts, explained the situation in Baghdad to the little ones, Olvido had dared to murmur: "Too far away." And then, turning her back on the object of our admiration, she had gone down the hall shaking her head angrily, holding a conversation with herself.

"They're probably not even Christians," she said then.

At first, and although the sudden change to our life saddened me, I didn't take Olvido's strange notions too seriously. The years seemed to have fallen all at once on the old woman's fragile body, on that back which was determined to curve more and more as the days passed. But a chance event ended up overloading the already charged atmosphere. To my young mind, it was just a coincidence; for my parents, it was a misfortune; for old Olvido, it was the confirmation of her dark intuitions. Because it happened next to the noisy faceless group, in front of the brass pendulum, facing the gold-plated hands. Matilde was polishing the little box which housed the Sun and Moon, the nameless stars that made up the diminutive parade, when her mind suddenly clouded over, she tried to grab hold of the scales with their sand, to steady herself on a nonexistent step, to prevent an inevitable fall. But the lightweight stepladder refused to support her oscillating body any longer. It was an accident, a feint, a momentary loss of consciousness. Matilde wasn't well. She'd said so in the morning when she was dressing the boys. She felt nauseous, her stomach turning, perhaps the previous night's supper, who knows, maybe a secret glass of something by the warmth of the fire. But there was no way to make oneself heard in that kitchen dominated by somber foreboding. And now it wasn't just Olvido. To the old woman's unnameable fears was added Matilde's spectacular terror. She prayed, exorcised, moaned. They seemed more united than ever before, murmuring ceaselessly, muttering unfinished sentences, swapping advice and prayers. The old rivalry, the competition between their respective arsenals of prodigals and ghouls, was now left well behind. It was as though the stories which had made us vibrate with emotion were nothing more than games. Now, for the first time, I felt that they were scared.

Throughout that winter I steadily delayed, little by little, my walk home from school. I stopped in empty squares, in front of cinema posters, I stared at the illuminated window displays on the main street. I put off as long as possible the inevitable contact with nights at home, suddenly sad, unexpectedly cold, although wood still burned in the hearth and from the kitchen came the smells of fresh bollos and popcorn. My parents, submerged for some time in preparations for a trip, didn't seem to notice the dark cloud that had entered our territory. And they left us alone. A world of old women and children. Going up the stairs in single file, holding hands, not daring to speak or to look at one another, to glimpse in someone else a spark of fear which, if shared, would force us to name what was nameless. And we went up step by step with our souls hunched, holding our breath on the little landing, hurrying up to the first-floor landing, pausing for a few seconds to catch our breath, counting in silence up the last few stairs, our hearts pounding in our chests with precise, rhythmic, perfectly synchronized beats. And once we reached our bedrooms, the old women tucked the little ones in, children who had forgotten their capacity for tears, their right to question, their need to invoke with words their unconfessed fears. Then they said good night, kissed each of us on the forehead and as I turned on a weak light next to the head of my bed I heard them drag their feet to their bedroom, open the door, chatter between themselves, complain, sigh. And then to sleep, not bothering to extinguish the dim glow from the naked light bulb, to dream unsettled dreams which shouted out the silenced motive for their waking worries, the Unnamed Lord, the Lord and Master of our ancient and infant lives.

My parents' absence lasted no longer than a few weeks, but long enough that when they returned they found the house aggravatingly different. Matilde had gone. A message, a letter from her village, an ailing sister who anxiously requested her presence. But how could it be? Since when did Matilde have sisters? She never mentioned her but she had a sister back in the village. Here was the letter: on squared paper a shaky hand explained the details of her unexpected departure. All they had to do was read it. That's why Matilde had left it: so that they'd understand that she did what she did because she had no other option. But it was a letter without a stamp. How had it got to the house? A relative had brought it. A man appeared at the door one morning, letter in hand. And this strange and affected style? My mother looked among her books for an old etiquette and society manual. Those notes of condolence, congratulations, change of address, communication of unfortunate circumstances. She had read that letter somewhere before. If Matilde wanted to leave them she didn't have to resort to ridiculous excuses. But she, Olvido, couldn't answer. She was tired, she felt ill, she had waited until they got back to declare that she was unwell. And now, lying flat out on the bed in her room, she desired nothing else but to rest, to be left in peace, to not be bothered with their efforts to get her to eat something. Her throat refused to swallow anything, not even a sip of water. When it was arranged that the little ones and I would go and spend a few days with some distant relatives and I went up to say good-bye to Olvido, I thought I was looking at a stranger. She had grown alarmingly thin, her eyes seemed enormous, her arms were bundles of skin and veins. She stroked my head almost without touching me, her face twisting into a grimace that she must have thought was a smile, adding to the scant words that blossomed from her lips with the brilliance of her gaze. "First I thought it had to happen sometime," she muttered, "some things start and others end . . ." And then, as if seized by an insurmountable fear, grabbing my plaits, trying to spit out something that had long been burning in her mouth and now began to burn my ears: "Stay safe. Protect yourself . . . Don't be caught off guard even for a moment!"

When I came home a week later I found a repulsively empty room, the smell of disinfectant and pharmacy cologne, the floor polished, the walls white-washed, not a single object or item of clothing in the wardrobe. And, at the far end, under the window that looked out onto the sea, all that was left of my beloved Olvido: a naked mattress, rolled up on the rusty springs of the bed.

But I hardly had time to suffer her absence. Calamity had decided to take it out on us, giving us no respite, denying us the rest that it became clear we urgently needed. Things fell out of our hands, chairs broke, food went off. We felt nervous, agitated, fretful. We had to make an extra effort, pay more attention to everything we did, take the greatest care in any activity no matter how simple and everyday it might seem. But even so, although we fought against that growing unease, I intuited that the process of deterioration to which the house had succumbed couldn't simply be halted with our best intentions. So often did we forget, so frequently were we careless, so incredible were the blunders we continually committed that now, looking back down the years, I see the tragedy that marked our lives as something logical and inevitable. I never knew if that night we forgot to remove the braziers, or if we did so too hurriedly, as with everything in those days, leaving behind the smallest ember hidden between the flaps of the folding table or among the tassels of some carelessly abandoned tablecloth . . . But we were dragged from our beds by the shouts and, wrapped in blankets, we feverishly descended the fearsome stairs that all of a sudden were filled with dense, black, choking smoke. And then at a safe distance, a few meters from the garden, we saw a gigantic and unforgettable spectacle. Purple, red, yellow flames, their glow blotting out the first light of day, competing among themselves to reach the highest, appearing through windows, crevices, skylights. There was nothing to be done, they said, everything was lost. And so, while immobilized by panic, we contemplated the hopeless fight against the fire, I felt as if my life would end at that precise moment, at only twelve years of age, wrapped in a murmur of laments and condolences, next to a house that had long stopped being my home. The cold of the blacktop made me curl up my feet. They felt disproportionately large and ridiculous, almost as much as the shins which stuck out of my too-short and too-small pajama bottoms. I covered myself with a blanket and then I heard the voice which dealt me the coup de grâce. It came from behind me, from among trunks and filing cabinets, objects saved at random, worthless paintings, bits of crockery, at best a couple of silver candlesticks.

I know that for the neighbors gathered on the Paseo it was nothing more than the inopportune chime of a beautiful clock. But to my ears it had sounded like sharp, treacherous, perverse laughter.

That same early morning the naive conspiracy of forgetfulness was plotted. Of life in the village we would remember only the sea, walks on the beach, striped summerhouses. I pretended to adapt to our new way of life but in the coming days I didn't miss a detail of everything that was said in my underappreciated company. The antiques dealer refused to take the clock back, alleging reasons of dubious credibility. The mechanism had deteriorated, the wood was worm-eaten, the dates falsified . . . He denied ever having possessed an object of such outlandish size and questionable taste, and he counseled my father to sell it to a scrap yard or get rid of it at the nearest dump. My family didn't obey the forgetful merchant, but they did, however, acquire his astonishingly calm manner in denying the obvious. Never again could I pronounce the forbidden name without fantasy, my overactive imagination or the innocent superstitions of old women being held to blame. But on San Juan night when we were leaving my childhood village for good, my father demanded that we stop the rental car near the main street. And then I saw it. Through the smoke, the neighbors, the children gathered around the bonfires. The flames hid the figures of the dancers, the clockwork pieces had come away from the casing and the face hung, inert, above the glass door which in other times had covered a pendulum. I thought of a giant whose throat had been slit and I shuddered. But I didn't want to let my emotions get the better of me. Remembering an old fondness, I half-closed my eyes.

She was there. Laughing, dancing, swirling around the flames together with her old friends. She played with the chains as though they were made of air, as if by merely thinking it she could fly, jump, join unseen in the children's joy, the din of the firecrackers and rockets. "Olvido," I said, and my own voice brought me back to reality.

I saw my father stoke the fire, fan the flames and return to the car, panting. When he opened the door he met my expectant eyes. Faithful to the law of silence, he said nothing. But he smiled, kissed me on the cheek and although I'll never have a chance to remind him of it, he held the back of my head so I would look straight forward and wouldn't dare to feel pity or sadness welling up.

That was the last time that, half-closing my eyes, I knew I saw them.

$$\mathbf{Ag} \xrightarrow[by]{trsltd} \mathbf{Fg}$$

from "Rage"

Antonio GAMONEDA
Translated by Forrest GANDER

from "Rage"

From violent dampnesses, from
places where the residues
of torments and whimpers mesh,
comes
this arterial grief, this shredded
memory.
They go insane,
even the mothers who run through my veins.

DE LAS violentas humedades, de
los lugares donde se entrecruzan
residuos de tormentas y sollozos,
viene
esta pena arterial, esta memoria
despedazada.
Aún enloquecen
aquellas madres en mis venas.

from "Rage"

The tortured shadows
near the signs.

I think about the day when horses learned to weep.

*HASTA los signos vienen
las sombras torturadas.*

Pienso en el día en que los caballos aprendieron a llorar.

Who shows up
shouting, announcing
such a summer, lighting
black lamps, hissing
into the pure blue of knives?

¿QUIÉN viene
dando gritos, anuncia
aquel verano, enciende
lámparas negras, silba
en la pureza azul de los cuchillos?

from "Rage"

They come with lanterns, lugging
blind snakes to
the albescent sand.

There's a blaze of bells. Steel
can be heard groaning
in the city surrounded by howls.

*VIENEN con lámparas, conducen
serpientes ciegas a
las arenas albarizas.*

*Hay un incendio de campanas. Se
oye gemir el acero
en la ciudad rodeada de llanto.*

They scream before calcined walls.

They note the silhouette of knives, see
the sun's circle, the surgery
of the animal stuffed with shadow.

They hiss
in the white fistulas.

GRITAN ante los muros calcinados.

Ven el perfil de los cuchillos, ven
el círculo del sol, la cirugía
del animal lleno de sombra.
Silban
en las fístulas blancas.

from "Rage"

There was an extraction of men. I saw
the root living on the omen.

I saw insects sucking up tears, saw
blood on the yellow churches.

*HUBO extracción de hombres. Vi
la raíz morada del augurio.*

*Vi a los insectos libando el llanto, vi
sangre en las iglesias amarillas"*

There were scorched flowers and denim
draped over a weeping machine.
Oil and shrieking in the steel and
propellers and bloody numbers
in the purity of my rage.

HABÍA flores abrasadas, dril
sobre la máquina que llora.
Aceite y llanto en el acero y
hélices y números sangrientos
en la pureza de la ira.

I recognized the tenanted shrouds
and the spark plugs of pain. Orations
boiled up between the lips
of frigid women.

CONOCÍ los sudarios habitados
y las bujías del dolor. Hervían
las oraciones en los labios
de las mujeres frías.

from "Rage"

It was
mortal music, the shriek
of incessant horses, it was
a funeral pavane at the hour
of the bloodied cotton ball.

It was the drooping of thousands of heads,
the gargoyle, its maternal howl, the circles
of the tormented hen.

It's even, once again, the whitewash, the bone
cold in our hands, the
policeman's black marrow.

FUE
la música mortal, el alarido
de los caballos incesantes, fue
una pavana fúnebre a la hora
del algodón ensangrentado.

Fue la declinación de mil cabezas,
la gárgola que aúlla maternal, los círculos
de la gallina atormentada.

Es aún, otra vez, la cal, el hueso
frío en nuestras manos, la
médula negra de la policía.

from "Rage"

I saw
bodies along the edge of
the cold acequias.

Shrouded
in light.

VI
cuerpos al borde de
las acequias frías.

Amortajados
en la luz.

I saw the ropes and cords, saw
the metallic seed and the briars
white with spines and light. Enpurpled,
they were gobbling up the insects.

VI los alambres y las cuerdas, vi
la semilla del metal y el soto
blanco de espinos y de luz. Con púrpura
se alimentaban los insectos.

from "Rage"

I found mercury in my pupils, tears
in the lumber, light
on the wall of the dying.

*HALLÉ mercurio en las pupilas, lágrimas
en las maderas, luz
en la pared de los agonizantes.*

Beneath the busyness of ants
there were eyelids and there was
toxic water in the gutters.

Even in my heart
there are ants.

*BAJO la actividad de las hormigas
había párpados y había
agua mortal en las cunetas.*

*Aún en mi corazón
hay hormigas.*

It's going to dawn over the prisons and tombs.
The tortured head eyes me: its
ivory blazes like caught lightning.

VA a amanecer sobre las cárceles y las tumbas.
Me mira la cabeza torturada: su
marfil arde como un relámpago cautivo.

Jez ——— Tb
trsltd
by

The Last Day on Earth

Juan EDUARDO ZÚÑIGA
Translated by Thomas BUNSTEAD

There seemed to be no one left in the barrio now and the windows were bare and the wind stirred through gates and the rats crossed noiseless rooms and the smell of the honeysuckle was fading. At night there were neither the cries of a sleepless child nor the clatter of dishes deep in the kitchens. In the gardens, it was not the sound of fountains but those of a dry, broken-off branch, a well's pulley creaking in the wind, an orphaned cat whispering an astonished meow and the acacias and jasmines, the lilacs and geraniums were hushed and gave their green light, indifferent to their forthcoming ruin. The detached houses that had once been their owners' every hope were now covered in dust; there was dust on the blue tiled staircases, dust on the moldings of the elegant façades, dust on the windowpanes and in the stairwells.

Those who had lived there and found happiness in the agreeable little gardens and those who had celebrated birthdays and watched their children grow old, all of them, one way or another, had left, giving in to the pressures of this new age and the barrio began to have no voices, was given over to gusts of wind, to the impacts of falling cornices, to the leaves eddying in corners with bits of paper that may have once been letters.

The murmuring on the far side of the barrio was neverending as the heavy machinery demolished homes, flattening and covering the soil with stone for the sidewalks and asphalt for the Gran Avenida designed for victory parades.

The barrio, once an agglomeration of family life, of modest comforts, of years of hard work and goals achieved, on finding itself in the path of the steamrollers and concrete mixers was irrevocably condemned. First, they would cut down the trees and shrubs, then the drains would be ripped out, the wrought-iron railings, the wooden beams and the demolition would quickly be underway, witnessed by no one.

A man and a woman were strolling along the acacia-lined streets. They were the last ones living there and they'd decided not to leave, not to abandon the place they'd lived together all these years. They decided not to accept moving to the apartment blocks where the noise and the improprieties would disturb their needed repose and intimacy. When the steamrollers did arrive, it would be more agreeable to die along with the barrio and all it represented.

Everything was ready for this last day and its imminence conferred a greater effusiveness on their words, their exchanges of opinion, their caresses and laughs; the days they were being deprived of would be taken in a trusting peace, full of beautiful reminiscences of all that had matured them, and a tacit forgetting of a civil war that had put paid to convictions and aspirations.

They strolled through the places they knew, remarking on the trivialities of solitude as well as the greenness of the gardens, which reached over the top of the railings without obscuring the view of the interior. Only one thing was unfamiliar to them, a noise; it could have been footsteps through dry branches and, coming closer to the house from which the noises were coming, they happened on a man in front of a tall bonfire with a mountain of papers crackling between barely visible flames turning into smoke. Books; from the gate they could see that it was books. The man was slowly opening them and tearing out the pages and throwing them on the fire.

The couple pushed on the gate, which creaked, and the man looked their way, holding their gaze for a moment and taking a few steps in their direction. As the mutual surprise lasted the couple contemplated the man: he was in his thirties or early forties, serious-looking and with an uncomprehending frown, and he was graying at the temples. As for his two observers, they were perhaps about the same age, a little older perhaps, and they had similarly attentive, watchful expressions, used to having to judge, and there was a touch of disappointment in their eyes.

No one said anything at first, but when they spoke their thoughts—their surprise at having found someone there, and making a fire—he explained that this was his house and these were his books. He was a little aloof and unsure but when the couple replied that they lived there too though they'd never encountered him, he came closer and asked how could this be if the barrio had been left empty and everyone had gone away, and seeing the two of them shrug, he smiled and said that that movement was his as well because he'd been prepared to disobey the orders, and that he'd come back to the place he'd lived in years ago and would oversee the final days of the house in which he'd been born. They moved closer to the bonfire and picked up a few of the books and saw some of their favorite authors and said it was a shame for them to be destroyed. He didn't know what to do with them; he thought no one was interested in such texts, and he felt the same about the old furniture and other mementos that were still in there and he motioned to the house. And so it was; when the three came inside, everything that might have been considered the comfort and adornment of a home had been placed in piles in the room. They became more and more curious with every object in this chaos: pictures, clothes, glass lamps, high mirrors, old chests . . . and passing through the spaces between these heaps prompted comments, meaning that they found out about one another's opinions and tastes. When they came back out into the garden where the bonfire had died down, the couple suggested the man come and eat with them.

Since they'd taken the final decision, the couple had been making exquisite meals and they'd amused themselves cooking sumptuous dishes and they'd bought the best wines. And in this first meal with the stranger they made clear the reason for such cares and he was only too happy to take part. And so they found that they could be friends and could share the final happiness that was the couple's proposition to themselves, and on hearing them explain precisely what this would consist of, he admitted that he had also decided to end when everything ended.

Amazed by the meeting and at such consonance—he was also one of the defeated from the civil war—and pleased to have come across a peer who was in such exceptional, identical straits, the couple kept him up into the night with their chatting. But the next day he shouted to them from the street and when he came into the garden they saw he'd brought them a present, an old gramophone that they hurried to turn on, playing record after record; it became clear that they were also equally lovers of music. At points, Caruso's voice or one of Chopin's waltzes appeared to awaken echoes in the neighboring gardens but if the mechanism ran down they'd hear complete silence and, faraway, the roar of the machines carrying on their ruinous advance.

The stranger suggested they come and live with him, saying they could have the run of the house and could uncover everything in the rooms with all his family memories in them.

The couple convinced him that it would be easier for him to come and live with them and just bring what he needed; they'd live together for as long as it was possible.

And this was how a shared life began, a life of doing only what pleased them, passing the long, hot summer's days in games, conversations, sharing meaningful silences, savoring the minutes that went by indifferent to what would come next, putting their minds to forgetting the calamities of the recent defeat.

They pooled their remaining money; when it ran out, they'd sell anything that was of any value and with the proceeds acquire on the black market whatever was required for their well-being. Halfway through the morning they made a succulent meal; the smell that came from the kitchen and that at midday would be carried on the air through the gardens attracted roving cats which watched at a distance as, in the shade of two leafy acacias, the trio would lay a long table with a white cloth, vases of flowers, dishes, and glasses for a long lunch.

The smiling stranger, whom they'd dubbed Falstaff, brought new and surprising things from his house every day to amuse the couple who, for their part, showed him stamp collections and talked him through the stories behind old family portraits and laughed at the rigid attitudes and the strictures of those past times.

After the meal they'd drink spirits whose high prices they'd had no qualms about paying and they'd read to one another—an author they all admired—and hours went by in commenting on these readings or making Falstaff, who had a lovely voice, recite poems that they all knew by heart.

Come the evening, when the air grew cooler, and by candlelight (the electricity had been cut off long ago) that gave both the rooms and their faces an aspect mysterious and new, they'd make music. Knocking the dust from violins and guitars and a xylophone, they improvised; the impulse of the unplanned rhythms joined with their voices and, out of tune, raspy from so much laughter, they sang in unison songs that they all also knew. The deep shadows cutting across their faces brought to mind the makeup used in Eastern theater and the next day they painted their faces and began making theater, with no audience, and with no backdrop other than the passing of their last days. New characters crossed between the stands of geranium: an Assyrian king, a medieval page of some sort, a fairy enveloped in gauze and tulle, in accordance with whatever they felt like dramatizing and with whimsical outfits that each chose from the chests in which, sixty or eighty years earlier, women who wanted to be desired had kept their long velvet dresses and opalescent blouses. The steps in the gardens were the preferred stage and there long soliloquies would be heard, interrupted by bursts of laughter and applause.

One afternoon, to the strains of a clarinet, a Salome appeared up on the balcony; she wore a resplendent multicolored robe and a silver mask that hid half her face and she declaimed these disconcerting words:

Jokanaan, I am amorous of thy body! Thy body is white like the lilies
of a field that the mower hath never mowed. Thy body is white like the
snows that lie on the mountains of Judaea. The roses in the garden of
the Queen of Arabia are not so white as thy body, nor the feet of the
dawn when they light on the leaves, nor the breast of the moon when
she lies on the sea, there is nothing in the world so white as thy body.

The arms reached out languid and undulating toward a Jokanaan who wasn't there, and meanwhile Falstaff, wearing breeches, a billowing shirt with damask trim, and a large beret stuck with several green feathers, cried out:

> What if it tempt you toward the flood, my lord,
> Or to the dreadful summit of the cliff
> That beetle o'er his base into the sea,
> And there assume some other horrible form,
> Which might deprive your sovereignty of reason
> and draw you into madness?

The clarinet sharpened its pace and Falstaff, seating himself on the steps, covered his face with his hands and feigned sobs:

> To be or not to be, that is the question.
> Whether 'tis nobler in the mind to bear
> The slings and arrows of outrageous fortune
> Or to take arms against a sea of troubles,
> And by opposing end them . . .

Salome came down the steps, opened her robes and exposed her body to him and bent down over Falstaff. He received her kisses and caresses, felt the weight of her legs on his and against the unyielding steps they slowly introduced their bodies to one another.

Long moments later, gusts of a warm wind arrived, the fluctuating music was still accompanying them and the magnificent clothes were being cast off and the beret rolled away and the two of them, for some minutes holding one another tightly and then, slackening and uncoupled, came slipping serenely down to the ground where they continued their play of love and the daylight began to fade. After, they lay still, breathing hard, their muscles soothed; they gazed at the sky through the leafy acacia canopy.

The clarinet had stopped, as if the musician reclining in his willow arm-chair was submerged in a like languor but when they got up from the ground and hurried over to the dry fountain and began pumping water on each other, he came down too, took off what little he'd been wearing, and the three of them washed, laughing, aiming the jet of water at one another and its cold silvery strike woke them from the evening torpor.

When they decided to go to sleep at midnight, Falstaff didn't retire to the room he'd been sleeping in before, rather they made the couple's bed wider and the three of them, in the half-light cast by a candle surrounded by dragonflies, gave themselves up to love's wise recourses. And finally slept, intermeshed as one body.

At sunrise the next day and upon lifting themselves out of sleep, they looked at one another with refreshed, affectionate looks, and with the passing of the following hours felt an intimate sense of contentment spread and this allowed them to be even more free in their relations, even more tender. Carried along by a greater vivacity, they embarked on new games in the gardens as well as conversations in which they recounted the best moments of their lives with unguarded sincerity. They'd gathered around themselves the products of intelligence and inventiveness, art and nature, and they partook of it all in an exceptional sphere where, fleetingly, they were able to identify pleasure and happiness and, possibly, also, forgetting; they studied engravings in books, they breathed in the antique smells of little jewelry boxes made of rare woods, they stretched out naked on silks and satin and they adorned themselves with attractive necklaces and flowers. From that night on, their appetite for food intensified, as well as for relating their dreams, and for distancing themselves from the unhappy past, and dressing up in the most audacious and extravagant manner and, at dinner, when the spirits and the wine had dropped fire in the three friends' souls, candlelit masks welled up out of the darkness, enhancing the splendid nudes.

One day they found that there was no longer any running water and realized that the machines were getting closer and that within a couple of days the custodians of the works would appear and that the three of them wouldn't be able to carry on giving themselves over to freedom.

They went out into the street and heard the roar of the demolition in nearby houses and the voices of the workers who were loading the trucks with the useless materials that had once been people's homes.

The end had come and they acknowledged it calmly and agreed that they couldn't put off the decision they'd made. They spent a little while wandering through the gardens and then went into the room they'd been using as a bedroom and where they'd gathered all the things that in their eyes were most beautiful and apt to go with them. Out of the wardrobe they took the dose they'd guarded so closely and they dissolved it equally in three glasses of wine that they drank in unison, without saying a word. They knew it would act quickly and they lay down on the bed; there, as a farewell, they embraced, shuddering with the emotion of the good-bye, and now came the first effects, contractions and a suffocating heat, and then they lost consciousness and the bodies lay inert on sheets that had been their companions.

They never knew that they hadn't been the only ones in the abandoned barrio and that their parties, banquets, and masquerades had been witnessed by three children who, day after day, had spied on them from behind the hedge and railings and, awed and amazed, watched how they enjoyed themselves, how they read to one another, how they played croquet and catch and how their voices intoned songs and laughter.

Two boys and a girl, listless friends who came from nearby streets, they'd wandered through the empty barrio and come across a house where people were doing something that made them feel envious and, hearing and seeing them, they'd felt attracted and whenever they could would hurry to that place and, hidden in the hedges, follow all the amazing things revealed by imagination and spontaneity.

But that day they were surprised to find the people not there and in the afternoon dared to enter the gardens and go up the steps and over the threshold into the house. There were no noises, no music, not a single voice. They tiptoed through the rooms and came to one and halted in the doorway; they saw them there, lying on a large bed, rigid, pale. There was a pile of furniture and pictures, books and bottles, lamps and bronze figurines and the three children saw themselves, horrified visitors, reflected in the large mirror. Their young intelligence grasped the truth of their discovery and without a word they started away but a shared thought stopped them; here, at their fingertips, was treasure.

They took a few cautious steps forward and began to gather the things they liked most. A hat, Salome's robes, some necklaces, stamp collections, an enormous box of sweets . . . and when their arms were full the trio left at a run, crossed the gardens and from the hedge checked to see if anyone was around, but everything was quite deserted.

The children fled to another barrio, one that in later years would perhaps come under the threat of a similar destruction and so they too, in solitude, would preserve a fragment of beauty, of love, of happiness, as they waited for the first day on earth.

$$\text{Imp} \xrightarrow[by]{trsltd} \text{AMc}$$

Social Skills

Ignacio MARTÍNEZ DE PISÓN
Translated by Anne MCLEAN

The Dodge Dart parked on the crosswalk with its right front wheel up on the curb and the fender touching the lamppost. Doña Mercedes, sitting in the passenger seat, opened the door and let out a snort.

"Your driving is getting worse and worse, Hija. You're really showing your age," she said, although Felisa was eighteen years her junior.

Felisa was Doña Mercedes's maid, cook and, when necessary, driver. Petite, somewhat hunched, with a mousy face, Felisa got out to take a look.

"It's not that bad," she said.

"You're getting more foolish by the day as well. Come on, help me."

It was help she asked for but Felisa had to do everything: open the back door, gather up poor Fosca, wrapped in her old tartan blanket, in her arms, and ring the veterinarian's doorbell with her elbow. Fosca, without moving a muscle, let out a gentle moan. They heard footsteps inside the clinic, and the old woman grabbed the dog and gestured to Felisa to go back to the car and find a place to park.

"Hurry, she's heavy," she said as the door opened to reveal the shining, round face of Laura Lumbreras, the vet's daughter.

Without giving her time to say a word, Doña Mercedes rushed into the waiting room and sat down on the sofa with the dog on her lap. The walls were decorated with photos of different breeds of dogs. Fosca, a mutt, rescued from the alley behind the house when she was just a puppy, didn't resemble any of those dogs. Doña Mercedes covered her nose with her handkerchief and cried a little:

"My poor Fosca, poor little Fosquita . . ."

Laura, babbling incoherent phrases, ran to alert her father, who soon took charge of the situation. Lumbreras was an affected and smarmy man, who looked a bit like an ultraconservative priest. He sat down beside the old lady and rubbed the damp muzzle of the dog, who slowly closed her eyes. There was something sterile and mechanical in his consoling words that took away some of his credibility.

"My dear Mercedes, my daughter told me that you'd called . . . We know, don't we: the moment eventually arrives for each of us, and for our beloved pets as well. It is a painful moment, but more for us than for them. Let's see. Swollen glands? Yes. Lesions, too. General decline, motor difficulties . . . Don't worry. She won't feel a thing. An injection, a little sleepiness that gets deeper and deeper, and that's it."

The dog, as if she knew they were talking about her, opened her eyes and looked at her owner, who choked back a sob.

"My poor little Fosquita . . ." she said once more. "She knows just what's going on."

"I know it's sad, but there's nothing else to do . . ."

Doña Mercedes grew philosophical:

"Death makes us all the same. Animals, people. People get a bit like animals and animals a bit like people, don't you think?"

The dog, with her big, limp ears and those clustered little teeth, had always been ugly, and was even more so now that she was ill.

"I think she understands what we're saying," the old lady went on. "If she started talking right now, it wouldn't surprise me. Can you imagine? Can you imagine her saying: why are you doing this to me, when I've always been so loyal, when I've always loved you, with all the moments of happiness I've given you over the last ten years?"

"Come, come now, my dear Mercedes . . ." said the vet, picking up the dog and cradling her like a baby.

The woman shook the tartan blanket and pushed it away from her. The gesture seemed to be all she needed to pull herself together.

"And what does one do with a dead animal?" she said, stuffing her handkerchief up her sleeve. "Where do we have to take it?"

"Don't you worry about that. We," and here he motioned in the direction of his daughter, who nodded with a grief-stricken air, "will take care of Fosca."

They both stood up.

"May I?" she asked, holding out the palm of her hand.

"Of course."

Doña Mercedes slowly, very slowly stroked the dog, who emitted another groan, perhaps her last.

"Many thanks. And send me the bill," said the old lady with a faltering voice.

Laura, folding the blanket, walked her to the door. Then she joined her father in the examination room. The dog was lying on a table beneath a strong white light. While looking through the drawers for his instruments, Lumbreras didn't even bother to strap down the animal, who didn't have the strength to move and seemed to have meekly accepted her fate. He placed a disposable syringe on the small aluminum auxiliary table and pulled on his latex gloves one finger at a time. Before breaking the seal of the syringe, he looked over the dog one last time.

"Fosca, Fosca . . ." he said.

He bent down over the dog's mammary glands and observed carefully. Then, looking at the ceiling, he felt them meticulously. Laura realized her father had just made an unexpected discovery.

"What do you think?" he asked, not expecting a reply.

The girl watched attentively. Lumbreras allowed several seconds to pass before saying:

"They're not tumors."

Another pause. This time it was Laura who interrupted it:

"What then?"

"It's milk."

"Milk?"

"Galactorrhea," the veterinarian nodded. "It tends to present in older dogs following estrum."

"And the motor difficulties?"

"Who knows. A bit of fever, some passing illness. . . it could be anything."

He nodded in the direction of the street.

"See if you can catch her. Tell her to come back."

Having seen how upset the old lady was, the simple idea of cheering her up put him in a good mood. While he killed time patting Fosca, he caught himself humming the drinking song from La Traviata. He heard some noise behind him and shouted:

"Come in, come in!"

Doña Mercedes, escorted by Laura, approached with a hesitant expression. The veterinarian didn't notice the fact that she did not have the tartan blanket with her.

"Come in!" he repeated.

The old lady looked shorter than she had a few minutes earlier. She stopped a few inches from the table and looked at the dog, who greeted her by weakly moving her tail and sighing almost inaudibly.

"Good news. What we have here is a pseudopregnancy. A phantom gestation, shall we say."

The silence that followed this declaration was just that: silence.

"What do you mean?" Doña Mercedes finally said.

"These things happen: sometimes the symptoms are so similar. . . Anyway, it's nothing. All better. She shouldn't eat anything for the next twenty-four hours, and keep her from licking herself because that stimulates the glands. . . Otherwise she's perfectly fine, and should live quite well for a few more years."

Lumbreras took off his gloves, snapping them in mid-air.

"Don't you understand, Doña Mercedes?" he went on, smugly. "We're not going to have to put Fosca to sleep. We'll put her back in the car right now and you can take her home."

The old lady, unexpectedly stern, said:

"I thought we'd made things clear. I've already said good-bye to her. Now do what you have to do."

She walked toward the exit, and didn't even stop as she added:

"And don't forget to send me the bill. Good afternoon."

Father and daughter looked at each other and then looked at Doña Mercedes, who had left the door open on her way out.

In the street, the Dodge was double-parked. Felisa, with her seat belt buckled, had to lean over and stretch her arm to unlock the door, which she then managed to open with her fingertips. To get into her seat, the old lady held onto the edge of the door with her right hand and the top of the seat with her left. As with all elderly people, it was harder for her to get into than out of a car (and harder to go down stairs than up). The operation was carried out in several stages. In between two of them she stopped a moment to say:

"You really are useless, Hija. You couldn't find a parking place this time either."

Felisa puffed out her cheeks and blew a raspberry. The old lady responded by slamming the car door.

"Home, right?" said Felisa.

"Where else?"

When they arrived, the house still smelled of the lunchtime lamb chops.

"Let's see if we can air the place out a little," said Doña Mercedes.

"That's up to you now. Not me."

Felisa's belongings were still where she'd left them that morning, piled up beside the umbrella stand in the front hall. Among them the imitation leather suitcase she'd bought thirty-four years earlier, when she was on the brink of leaving the house to marry a locksmith who turned out to be a good-for-nothing. Around the suitcase were several cardboard boxes filled with various objects. Some of them contained clothes, almost all hand-me-downs from Doña Mercedes, who never threw out a garment without offering it to Felisa first.

In another was a selection of tin bas-reliefs, from back when the two women would devote rainy afternoons to handicrafts. In another were framed photographs: photos of Felisa with her family before going into service, photos of her sister's wedding in the village church, photos of her nephews and nieces when they were babies or when they took their First Communion, a photo of the oldest swearing allegiance to the flag, another of the next oldest on honeymoon in Florence. . . They were photos of a possible life, and beside them were few, very few photos of her real life, her life with Doña Mercedes, always reluctant to pose in front of a camera.

"A whole life . . ." sighed Felisa, and then, to make the comment seem less serious, softly sang: "A whole life long I'll be spoiling you . . ."

Doña Mercedes walked into the room they called the study and that, since the death of her husband, sixteen years before, had been collecting all the bits of junk that had fallen out of favor in the rest of the house. There, behind a broken sewing machine and an old stationary bicycle, was the chest of drawers in which they kept important papers. From the top drawer she took out a bankbook and a small folder. When she got back to the front hall, Felisa was coming out of the bathroom. The sound of the tank filling up came to an end, as always, with a somewhat anxious gurgle. She held out the bankbook, open to the middle page.

"This is the last entry. Everything's in order, isn't it?"

Felisa, like a shy little girl, looked down at the floor. Doña Mercedes handed her the folder as well.

"The car is now in your name. And the insurance, paid up till June."

"And why would I want that gas guzzler?" whined the other woman.

She began to load her things into the trunk of the Dodge. The boxes that didn't fit ended up on the back seat.

"And you said you'd never fit everything in . . .!" the old lady reproached her from the front step.

There was still room in the front, and Doña Mercedes ordered her to go to the kitchen and get the basket of greengages to take.

"The whole basket?"

"The whole thing. You love those plums!"

Felisa obeyed and then stood beside the Dodge not really knowing what to do.

"Do you need anything? Do you want me to leave your dinner ready?" she finally said.

Doña Mercedes shook her head and gestured toward the sky as if to say: Get going now if you want to arrive before dark. Felisa waited a few seconds more to see if her employer was thinking of giving her a hug or saying a word or two of farewell. Seeing that she didn't make the slightest movement, she climbed in behind the wheel of the Dodge and rubbed her moist eyes.

"Call me when you get there," the old lady said then. "I don't like that high-way one bit."

The engine started and the car soon disappeared around the corner by the nun's nursery school. Doña Mercedes closed the door, then went to the little parlor that overlooked the back garden and sat down in her rocking chair to wait.

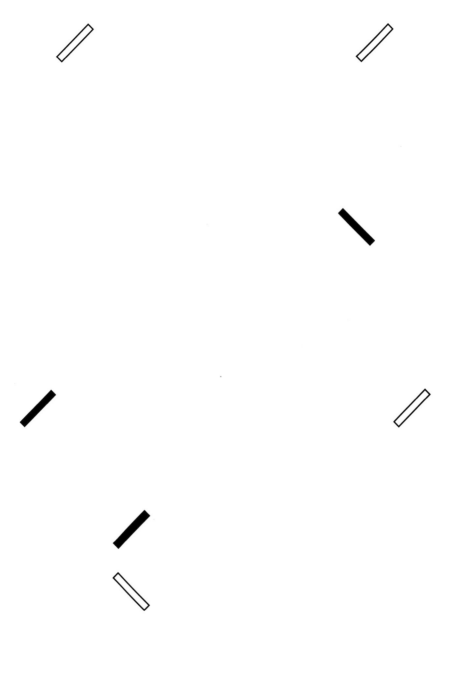

JAmr ———— Ss
trsltd
by

They Destroyed Our Radios and Televisions

Juan Antonio MASOLIVER RÓDENAS
Translated by Samantha SCHNEE

They destroyed our radios and televisions
to leave us without images,
without those maudlin songs
that lulled our past to sleep
back when we still believed in trains
by the seaside, at the ranch where Laura
carried her milk churns to the river
to meet the prince on horseback,
kissing the stamping steed on the mouth
like in Gwendolyn's garden,
abandoned to what they called love.
They made us spend nights
reading Barthes and Derrida
until words came undone
in our hands and nothing had more value
than what it could have had but never did
as if promises and the past
were one and the same. We could only
love dead women, on screens
they appeared naked and desolate, the most beautiful
was the one whose body was covered in down,
a dead child at her breast.
Our eyes beheld only grief.
Our ears heard only
strident, shouted words.
No one wanted to awaken us. They denied us
the orchards, the cities with taverns
and carriages, the peacefulness of cemeteries,
the hearses shining in the sun,
heads inclined before the deceased
and at the hour of the Angelus, the reaping
and the drunkenness of the grape harvest,
haylofts where someone finally
gave us their naked body
and the revelation made us cry.

Laura was still a virgin. Her children
not yet crying in the garden.
She greeted the crew of the Thetis
anchored on the River Ouse, she traversed
the undulating profile of the hills
of Sussex, beauty immersed

Nos destrozaron las radios y los televisores
para que nos quedásemos sin imágenes,
sin aquellas empalagosas canciones
que adormecieron nuestro pasado
cuando aún creíamos en los trenes
junto al mar, en el rancho donde Laura
iba con sus cántaras de leche al río
a encontrarse con el príncipe a caballo,
besando la boca del caballo que piafaba
como en el jardín de Güendalina
entregados a lo que ellos llamaban amor.
Nos obligaron a pasar las noches
leyendo a Barthes y a Derrida
hasta que las palabras se deshacían
en nuestras manos y nada tenía más valor
que el que pudo tener y jamás tuvo,
como si promesas y pasado
fuesen una misma cosa. Sólo podíamos
amar a las mujeres muertas, en las pantallas
aparecían desnudas y desoladas, la más bella
era la del cuerpo cubierto de vello
con un niño muerto en el pecho.
Nuestros ojos sólo veían dolor.
Nuestros oídos sólo escuchaban
palabras estridentes, chillidos.
Nadie quiso despertarnos. Nos negaron
los vergeles, las ciudades con tabernas
y carruajes, la placidez de los cementerios,
los carruajes negros brillando bajo el sol,
las cabezas inclinadas ante el difunto
y a la hora del ángelus, la siega
y la ebriedad de las vendimia,
los pajares donde alguien finalmente
nos entregaba su cuerpo desnudo
y la revelación nos hacía llorar.

Laura todavía era virgen. Sus hijos
todavía no lloraban en el jardín.
Saludaba a los tripulantes de Thetis
anclado en el río Ouse, recorría
el ondulante perfil de las colinas
de Sussex, belleza inmersa

in beauty, until in Newhaven
she discovered sea mist, a hairy
hand digging into her thighs,
violating her without her knowing
the love she no longer believed in,
nor would ever. All women expelled
from Paradise, condemned and abandoned,
become prostitutes. Don't humiliate
the humiliated, stop wounding
the dead, don't profane
beauty. The Sistine Chapel
is full of graffiti, the pope
has been dragged through the streets
of Rome, flogged by the boys
whom he so loved and caressed.
On computer screens
we search for our forgotten
identity, computers are our memory,
they return the past to us. Our mother,
a whore who fled the house
shortly after birthing me. She didn't like my face,
it wasn't telegenic, would never advertise
soap, happy among bubbles. She didn't want
to ruin her breasts. At night
she emptied her milk into the toilet
and I was awoken by hunger
and the bitter scent of her nipples.

And now I search for Laura, but she died,
crucified. Her virginity
offended men. And
before the cross they exposed her
naked, covered in blood
where we love women most
to make us stop loving them.
Until they abandoned us
in this wasteland which, from afar,
looked like an unreal city,
the Paradise in which
we ought never to have believed.
The open ground was filled
with the rotting cadavers of angels

en la belleza, hasta que en Newhaven
descubrió la bruma, una mano
velluda que hurgaba en sus muslos,
violándola sin que ella hubiese sabido
qué era el amor en el que ya no creyó
jamás. Todas las mujeres expulsadas
del Paraíso, vituperadas y abandonadas,
convertidas en prostitutas. No humilléis
a los humillados, dejad de herir
a los muertos, no profanéis
la belleza. La capilla Sixtina
está llena de graffiti, al Papa
lo han arrastrado por las calles
de Roma, azotado por los niños
a los que tanto quiso y acarició.
En las pantallas de los ordenadores
buscamos nuestra olvidada
identidad, ellos son nuestra memoria, nos
devuelven el pasado. Nuestra madre,
una meretriz que huyó de casa
apenas parirme. No le gustó mi rostro,
no era televisivo, nunca anunciaría
jabones, feliz entre pompas. No quería
estropearse los senos. Por las noches
vaciaba la leche en el retrete
y a mí me despertaba el hambre
y el olor acre de sus pezones.

Y ahora busco a Laura, pero murió
crucificada. Su virginidad
ofendía a los hombres. Y
antes de la cruz la expusieron
desnuda, cubierta de sangre
donde más amamos a las mujeres
para que dejásemos de amarlas.
Hasta que nos abandonaron
en este páramo que a lo lejos
parecía una ciudad irreal,
el Paraíso en el que nunca
deberíamos haber creído.
El descampado estaba lleno
de cadáveres putrefactos de ángeles

and, when an invisible hand opened the
doors, we heard the music
one hears in Heaven
but there was no one, no
path to follow, nothing
to remember. I had to invent
my past, this story I write
knowing it's not certain
because certainty doesn't exist.
I invent Laura and she flees.
Condemned to imagination,
cursed by her, I ignore
when the end of days will come,
when dawns will emerge
in this terrifying darkness.
I know, because I have just finished inventing it,
Laura is all women,
her pubic hair, her armpits,
her back where lizards repose,
her blank stare where the sun sleeps.
When I return to the world, will I remember
this story? Will I remember the one who was
mother, the violated woman, the desired woman,
the breath of beauty which now
denies me for all time? The threatening
commencement of Genesis, its evil
vegetation?

y, al abrirnos las puertas una mano
invisible, escuchamos la música
que se escucha en el Cielo
pero no había nadie, ningún
camino que seguir, nada
que recordar. Tuve que inventarme
mi pasado, esta historia que escribo
sabiendo que no es cierta
porque no existe la certeza.
Me invento a Laura y huye.
Condenado a la imaginación,
maldecido por ella, ignoro
cuándo se acabarán los días,
cuándo empezarán los amaneceres
en esta pavorosa oscuridad.
Sé, pues lo acabo de inventar,
que Laura ha sido todas las mujeres,
el vello de su pubis, sus axilas,
su espalda en la que duermen los lagartos
su mirada ciega en la que duerme el sol.
Cuando regrese al mundo, ¿recordaré
esta historia? ¿Recordaré a la que fue
madre, la mujer violada, la mujer deseada,
al aliento de belleza que ahora
se me niega para siempre? ¿El amenazador
principio de Génesis, su perversa
vegetación?

$$\textbf{Bv} \xrightarrow[by]{trsltd} \textbf{Dh}$$

The Devil Lives in Lisbon

Berta VIAS
Translated by Daniel HAHN

On Mondays Mother always got up at five o'clock. She would leave half an hour after getting out of bed, once she had gathered up all the breakfast crockery, and then, looking at us again with a smile, she would not be back home till Saturday. When she'd come back down the same path that she had gone up on Monday. Nieves was seven at the time. I was six. Elisa, just three.

Mother worked as a schoolteacher. In La Comba, a small village in the mountains. The little bus would come to fetch her every Monday at the end of the path, the one with the chestnut trees, by the beech forest. There, in La Comba, she had a room that she rented for the whole week. And they gave her lunch and dinner right there. Breakfast, too. The owner of the house and his oldest son worked in the mine. His wife looked after the little ones, the cows, the pastures and the vegetable garden, as well as feeding the family and the schoolteacher who would arrive each Monday from Pola de Siero. And during that time the three of us would be left in the care of our aunt. We saw even less of our father then.

There were some weeks when Mother would take us with her. Just one of the three of us. But that was right near the beginning, when we weren't yet in school, though sometimes, after we'd started at nursery, on turning four, Mother would make an exception and let us go with her, allowing us to miss class. Those weeks were like a great party for us. A party that we shared only with our mother, while all the others were left behind, down below in the town.

And so Elisa seemed to us to be the favorite, but it was really because in those days when we had to go to school, she was still very little and hadn't even started nursery. When she spent the week with Mother she would run around in the fields, milk the cows, bathe in the stream, and eat all the fruit she wanted. Sour cherries. Apples. Pears. Even figs. And it was not that we didn't have them here in town, it was that things tasted different there.

But there were some Saturdays when Mother did not return. It tended to coincide with the first Saturday of the month. Though not of every month. And right from the Monday, we—Nieves and I, perhaps even Elisa—knew it, because on those mornings she would be carrying a travel bag hanging over her shoulder and wearing a smile that was wider than usual, so wide that it made her look like a foreigner, a confident tourist, game for anything, arriving at a place she had dreamed of her whole life. The place many of us never reach.

And so Mother would walk away. The shadows from the chestnut trees playing on her shoulders. She would smile as she walked. In the rain. Or the sun. It was all the same. She walked like in the poem. Serene. Rapt. Glowing. Was it Prévert? Or Aragon? Perhaps Nieves would know. Or Mother, yes. Mother would definitely remember.

We also knew because on those weeks, when she disappeared, the hand-mirror disappeared, too, the one she always kept on top of the chest of drawers. In her bedroom. The only slightly showy object in the whole house. A house of whitewashed walls. Of large, old, simple pieces of furniture, worn with use and the passing of time.

The smile on those Mondays, Mother's smile as she disappeared amid the chestnut trees, was the smile of someone who has received instructions for a mission, of someone who feels protected, transported by a single word. Father, however, noticed nothing at all. Or at least, he seemed not to notice. Or acted as though he didn't see. As though he didn't care. All he needed were his endless card games, the binges he'd go on with his buddies. And when Mother left with that bag and that smile, we would stay nearly an extra forty-eight hours with our aunt, linking one week to the next, barely seeing her, just for a moment, in the kitchen, when in the early hours of Monday morning she set about her climb back up to La Comba.

Where was it that she went on those two days that seemed so endless to me? For those hours we all felt as eternal? Perhaps even father, too. For those days when I would always run, as perhaps my sisters Nieves and Elisa did, too, over to her bedroom, to consider the empty space left by the mirror. That mirror framed in complicated gold filigree, with a long, narrow handle, that Mother had inherited from old Aunt Freditas. Fredesvinda, her name was.

Where was it that she went? I don't know. I don't know where Mother would go off to. I'm not sure. All I know is that each time she came back, she told us she'd been somewhere different, some place new, in a different city, not too far away but exotic to our ears that were used only to the sparse sounds of the town. Whereas now, so long afterward, I think it was always the same place, one city, although I'm also not altogether sure which one. It's just a hunch.

One fine day, much later, Mother started to miss those appointments. Or were they merely trips, and, therefore, nothing like the rituals with which I imagined she distanced herself from the tedious, gray life she lived in the town, with Father? Today, a bit more than twelve years on, having seen that smile of hers from those days again, I think I have been able to establish where it was she went.

Mother, do you believe in God, Elisa asked her this afternoon. Mother smiled and answered her, as usual, with another question. And what about the devil? Do you believe in the devil? My sister looked at her, puzzled. Perhaps she had got goosebumps, like me. Perhaps her hair was standing on end, like mine. Perhaps even Nieves was feeling the same. Could it be that we still believed in the existence of The Evil One? Or was it because of the expression we recognized in our mother's face?

And Mother explained. José María used to say—do you remember him, one of my students from up there, in the mining village?—he used to say that the devil must be living in Lisbon. That's what he said in a fine essay that he wrote for me. Naturally he got a high mark that time, too. He was my favorite, after all. And the time I asked them to write down the name of one of the apostles, can you guess whose name José María wrote? Father Pío!

The three of us laughed. Nieves, who has already turned nineteen. Me, about to turn eighteen. And Elisa, who's only fifteen. Father Pío was the parish priest of La Comba. A good man, but with a temper on him like a thousand demons. Just think! And the thing with the *autos sacramentales* Do you remember? He thought they were the cars used by Popes, bishops, and senior priests.

José María must have imagined Lisbon as a magnificent place to live. That is probably why he thought of posting the devil there. Though he may have had a mistaken idea of what the city was like. And that's what I think, speaking as someone who also believes it must be the best place to live. What's certain is that the poor boy has never been there himself. Nor have I ever been in Lisbon, either. He at most would have come down here occasionally. To La Pola. And what of the devil? Could he know what or who the devil is?

And what became of little José María?, Nieves asked then. With an imagination like that, he should have become a writer. The poet of La Comba. He ended up at the mine, like everyone else, said Mother with a look of uneasy resignation.

Just imagine, Juan, in Lisbon, she said not long after that, turning toward me and tickling the back of my neck. Just like then, I now recall. On those Mondays when Mother had decided to leave on one of her trips, while we had our breakfast milk and bread, she would play with our hair, putting her fingers on the back of our neck and running them up to the crown of the head and ruffling our hair. We particularly liked that affectionate gesture, but soon understood that it was the prelude to her going away and received it with a bitter gladness.

Smiling, Mother suddenly exclaimed: Satan living in Lisbon. With that smile of twelve years earlier. The one from those Mondays when she'd walk away with her bag hanging over her shoulder. Glowing. Rapt. Serene. And I thought I saw in her eyes the fleeting passing of flowers, the reflection of bottles of wine. "Green wine," like they call it in Portugal, Mother? Yes, like your eyes. A transparent green. Like the glass of one of those bottles.

It almost felt as though I could feel her heart beating. Racing slightly. Then nostalgia clouded over them, her eyes. Like the mist of the sea when it wraps itself around cities, those cities you always feel far away from, even when you arrive there. The light of sadness was illuminating her face. And Mother shivered, as if she were feeling cold, sitting beside me on the bench, her tired old back leaning up against the wall of the house, against the stones that at this time in the evening were giving off the heat of the sun that they'd been storing up all day long. Mother shivered from head to toe, perhaps because she knew those secret days would never be returning.

Would she go to Lisbon? And would Madame see the devil there? I pictured a hotel room. Always the same one. And a table at a café. Perhaps that, too, was always the same. Walks among strangers along steeply sloping alleyways. Races to the platform on a station with tile-covered walls. And siestas on a beach. Fire and water at your feet, running over your body, your fresh skin covered in sand. Alone? With a girlfriend? Or with the devil?

And I was jealous of him. Yes, jealous of the devil. And of her. Of my mother. And angry at Father. Always hunched over a wooden table, the wood covered in cuts. The cuts that he used to make with his penknife. With a concentration of absolute rage. And stained. Stained by grease and fire, from the hot base of the saucepans, stains which were impossible to get rid of. And Father with the deck of cards constantly in his hands. Bright and dirty, the corners worn.

You were, and still are, an intelligent, determined woman. Hardworking. Tireless. And at the same time, you seemed to be filled with knots, as though you were always at a crossroads, about to enter the sanctuary of your dreams. To leave forever. Sweet and accessible at the same time. Why didn't you leave him, Mother? Why have you remained tied to this destiny, to a man you certainly no longer loved, and who probably didn't love you either? Who had never loved you as you deserved. Eternal love only lasts four months, that's what he used to say. Our father. And the other kind, two years, he would pronounce immediately afterward. Always so destructive, that sense of humor he had.

Was it because of us, Mother? Losing you would have been hard, but I would have liked to remember you always with that smile. Not to have you stroking our necks except in our dreams. There was this suicidal wish I had in which I imagined losing you, I've had it ever since I was a boy. Your being lost in another land. In other arms. With your smile. A smile to drive a man crazy. To drive men crazy. All of them.

Mother, did you drive men crazy? I'm sure you did, that you'd be able to do it still. Able to, without even putting your mind to it. Perhaps even driving yourself crazy, too. So did you drive men crazy? Or did you find yourself a man who was mad for love, whom you were too afraid to follow? And what if it was all just my imagining? And in reality you never were in Lisbon? Nor ever in the arms of the devil? And what if, after all, the devil never existed?

No. You've seen him, face to face. I know it. And that is why the mirror is broken now. In there, on top of the chest of drawers, in your bedroom. It's been there for years. Never moving. You probably never even look into it any more. Perhaps for fear of capturing an image that was lost in some corner of the past. The devil's reflection, suspended there in the void. Would it be there? In the mirror? And as for me, when I see that split in the glass, from one side to the other, my soul aches. This soul that I would have been ready to sell if it meant you would be able to leave here for ever.

Now, when winter returns and the chestnut trees lose their leaves, when the house falls silent and the windows are drenched with rain, we are the ones who will have to leave. And Elisa, as usual, the youngest, the one who looks most like you, will stay behind. Her green eyes, frank and alert, will stay with you for longer. Though you never know. Perhaps she will be the first to run into the devil. A proper, honest-to-God devil. And then she will walk away. Like you, smiling. Serene, rapt, glowing. Remember that, Mother.

$$\text{Pz} \xrightarrow[\text{by}]{\textit{trsltd}} \text{MFl}$$

Don't Do It

Pedro ZARRALUKI
Translated by Mara Faye LETHEM

He left his car in the parking lot of the hospital complex. It had all been under construction for years. Around him were unfinished buildings with display windows still protected by tape beside other old, dusty ones, with air conditioning units hanging off them like enormous ticks. Amid the buildings were pre-fab sheds, cranes, fenced-in areas all around, but he knew his route well. He passed a row of oleanders that had been relegated to no-man's-land, and he emerged in an open stretch where they usually parked the trucks that supplied the oxygen tanks. Hospital workers went there to smoke, since it was somewhat out of the way. They huddled in groups, all in white lab coats.

Miguel avoided looking at them. He continued on his way, quickening his step slightly, and soon he reached a brick building with large, narrow windows that looked more like vents. Beside the door was a plaque that read: PSYCHIATRY WARD. And beneath that: ADDICTIVE BEHAVIORS UNIT. He pushed the door and entered a wide foyer and found only a security guard sitting at a metal desk, doing a crossword puzzle in the newspaper and making the pen dance between his fingers. He didn't even look up when Miguel crossed the foyer and rang the bell. A young nurse appeared and led him to a small room. There she weighed him, took his blood pressure and asked him to blow into a machine that Miguel hated. She jotted down the results of it all on an index card.

Soon after, Miguel went into the psychiatrist's office. He sat in front of her and put the test results down on her desk. The doctor picked up the card by one corner carefully, as if trapping a butterfly by one wing, and glanced at it.

"You've been smoking, Miguel," she said to him. "It's at five, over the limit."

"It's this city that's over the limit," he answered. "I haven't had a cigarette in two months."

He wasn't lying. He felt uncomfortable and looked to one side. The walls were covered in white tiles. There was a divan in one corner. The first day he came there he'd thought that, lying on that divan, he'd have to explain to that doctor, who'd just turned fifty, how he had a teenage daughter with a woman he hadn't seen in a long time, and that they'd sent him to her unit because he'd had a mild heart attack. But she had never had him lie down on the divan.

"You've gained three kilos," he heard her say. "One more and we'll be at ninety. We are going to have to watch what we eat a little."

The psychiatrist was scrawny, with somewhat gaunt cheeks. It bugged Miguel that she spoke about his excess weight in the plural, as if she were including herself to make him feel they were in this together. It was clear the woman had never been fat or smoked. He had the impression, as he always did when he went there, that she'd never be able to help him. Not her and not anyone.

"Let's see, Miguel. How are you feeling?"

"Fine," he said. And he looked her in the eyes for a second.

"Are you constipated?"

Miguel shook his head.

"Sleeping poorly? Nightmares? Do you wake up anxious?"

Miguel shifted in his chair. The word anxious makes him anxious. And, he never could stand being asked how he was doing, when bumping into someone on the street. It was something that made him suddenly ill at ease.

"I sleep soundly," he said. "I take the pills you prescribed."

"And your mood? How do you feel?"

"Sad," he answered without any hesitation. "But that's nothing new."

"What do you mean?"

Miguel looked at the doctor again, but he couldn't bear the tranquility she was trying to transmit to him. He looked away.

"That doesn't have anything to do with smoking. I've been sad ever since I can remember."

For a second he thought that, finally, he had earned the divan. But he was wrong. He wasn't there for psychotherapy, just to treat his nicotine addiction.

"I think you should take an antidepressant," said the doctor.

That was exactly what Miguel didn't want to hear. As he understood it, antidepressants couldn't be mixed with alcohol.

"I can't," he answered. "I have high blood pressure. Besides, they haven't yet come up with a pill that can change the way I am."

"You're mistaken about that." The doctor opened up a folder and pulled out a sheet of paper that she looked at carefully. She brought a finger to her mouth and ran it along her lips as she seemed to vanish inside herself.

/

It was a little past nine when Miguel left her office. Too early to go to work, but he didn't have anything better to do. He thought about making some cuttlefish and peas. Miguel had a small restaurant. He cooked and took care of everything, except for waiting on the tables. A Dominican woman came in during serving hours to help him with that. She also took care of the espresso machine. She kept it so clean that it looked like it'd never been used but, every once in a while, it released some steam with a snort, like a locomotive about to depart.

He left the hospital complex, bought a newspaper, and paged through it as he drank an espresso with milk. Then he went back to the parking lot for his car. It was an old car, with one back door dented by a blow from a van. In the past he had used it to travel with his wife, when they still lived together and the girl was small. Now he had the feeling that he and that rusting pile of junk were declining at the same rate. They both smelled the same, a mix of sweat and overheated plastic.

He double-parked in front of the fishmonger's. He bought four large cuttlefish and put the bag in the trunk. He had just sat down in front of the steering wheel again when his cell phone rang. He struggled to extend his leg so he could get the phone out of his pocket, then brought it to his ear.

"I'm having a problem with Mom." It was his daughter's voice, high-pitched and fast like a bird's trill. "I'm furious."

"Good morning, Yolanda," answered Miguel.

"What's good about it? Tomorrow The Sounds are playing at the Apolo, and Mom won't buy me a couple of tickets. She says I should ask you for them. Fact is she's been unbearable lately. If this keeps up I'm coming to live with you."

"Calm down." Miguel looked around him, afraid a patrol car would pass and see him talking on the phone in the car. He wondered what his ex-wife spent the child support he sent her on. "I'll buy them for you."

"You can get them from a cash machine. But you have to go right now, Daddy. I hear they're selling out."

\

On the way to the restaurant he stopped the car again to buy the tickets. He put them in his shirt pocket and drove on. When he was getting close, he started to look for parking. He was lucky that day. He found a spot almost right in front of his restaurant's steel shutter. He opened the glove compartment to get the keys.

That was when he saw a girl leaning against a tree. She had long legs and her arms clasped behind her back. Their eyes met for perhaps too long of a second. Miguel didn't look away fast enough, making the girl think he was interested. She peeled herself off the tree somewhat apathetically and went over to his car. She stopped beside Miguel's door, a hand resting on the windshield. Miguel lowered the window and the girl crouched down to look it him. She was very young and had black eyes.

"Let me guess what you need," she said to him. "A little blowjob to start the day off right."

Miguel thought of the psychiatrist and how she had been so insistent about the antidepressant. He thought how that prostitute, in her own way, also seemed worried about improving his mood. Since he was slow to respond, the girl rested her elbows on the open window.

"I need you to move out of the way," Miguel said. "I need to go to work and I have to get out of the car."

The girl brought her shoulders together a bit so that the neckline of her blouse bulged. She had small pointy breasts, thick pink nipples. Miguel couldn't help looking at them. He felt his heart rate increase.

"Where do you work?" she asked.

"In a restaurant," answered Miguel, feeling unbearably docile. "Right here." And he pointed to the lowered shutter of his business.

The girl's eyes lit up.

"So you could treat me to a sandwich," she said. "I'm so hungry my stomach is growling."

Miguel looked at her with surprise. The girl finally moved away from the car door and he was able to get out. Once he was standing on the sidewalk he looked at her again. She was smiling. At first glance she seemed to be his height, but she was wearing very high heels. Even though she was too thin, she had a nice figure. Maybe not even twenty years old.

"What's your name?" asked Miguel.

The girl bit her lower lip, pensively. Then she smiled again, this time with a slightly adopted sassiness.

"Today I'll be Russian," she answered. "I'm Natasha."

"I'll make you a ham sandwich."

He went to the back of his car and pulled the bag of seafood out of the trunk. Then he headed toward the restaurant. Behind him he heard the girl's high heels against the sidewalk. When he got to the metal shutter he put the bag down on the sidewalk and knelt to open the lock. The girl extended an arm and spread the bag's handles to see what was inside.

"What is that?" she asked.

Miguel was already raising the shutter. As he did he felt a stabbing pain in his kidneys and stopped halfway.

"Cuttlefish," he said, bringing a hand to his side. "I stew them with peas and potatoes."

"Yuck!" she exclaimed. "I wouldn't eat that for anything in the world."

They entered the restaurant, bending down so they wouldn't hit their heads on the shutter, and Miguel flicked on the light switch. The tables were already prepared for lunch. The Dominican woman set them before she went home, while Miguel finished tidying up the kitchen. Then they said good-bye at the door and she headed toward the bus stop. She had been working with him for more than a year, but Miguel didn't know where she lived. He had never asked. The Dominican woman knew that Miguel had quit smoking. She realized the first day, when she arrived to wait on the lunch tables and saw there was no smoke in the restaurant. She went into the kitchen and congratulated him. She confessed that she'd been worried about his health.

The prostitute moved among the tables, stroking the tablecloths that covered them with a fingertip. Miguel, still at the door, observed her elegant, bony shoulders, the soft curves of her hips, her calves, tensed by the high heels. He hesitated for a moment.

"Natasha," he said. She turned. "I'm going to have to lower the shutter. I don't want someone to come in here and see you."

"Sure," answered the girl. "Do you have some water?"

The exertion gave Miguel another jab that left him with a feeling of warmth in his midsection. He went to the office, got the espresso machine going, and grabbed a small bottle of water. He put it on the counter, beside a glass. Then he went into the kitchen, placed the bag of cuttlefish in the sink, and prepared a ham sandwich. He rubbed a lot of tomato into the bread, which was a little dry. When he went out to the dining room again he found the girl sitting at a table. She had moved aside a table setting to be able to lift up a corner of the tablecloth. She didn't want to dirty it.

"The bread is from yesterday," said Miguel, putting the plate with the sandwich down in front of her. "My delivery doesn't come until later on."

"No problem. I really appreciate it."

The girl began to eat. She took big bites, stopping only to drink water straight from the bottle. Miguel stood stock still, watching her. He didn't know what to say.

"Did you finish school?" he finally asked. He instantly felt ridiculous for having said it.

The girl made a world-weary expression.

"I dropped out of high school," she answered. As she spoke a few crumbs flew from her mouth. "Now I'm supposedly studying to be a secretary, but I don't go to class. My boyfriend drops me off at the school every day, on his motorcycle. I wait until he drives off and I split."

"Does he know how you spend your days?"

"No, no way." She was silent for a moment, her brows knitted, as if trying to concentrate or imagine something. And then, in the tone of someone who has found the answer to a complicated question, she added, "He'd go nuts. He's very jealous."

She ate the last bite of sandwich. Then she stood up and approached Miguel. She caressed his chest with both hands.

"Now let's get down to us," she said, lowering her voice to a purr.

Miguel's heart rate shot up again. Don't do it, he said to himself, don't do it. He wanted to move away from her, but his legs didn't respond. His jaw started shaking intensely. He looked with fear at the lowered shutter. He hadn't locked it.

The girl kneeled before him. She brought her hands to his belt buckle. Miguel closed his eyes when his pants began to slide down to his ankles. Then his underwear. He felt a bit dizzy.

"You've got a really nice one," said the girl's voice. "Honestly, it's much better-looking than you. I think I'm going to ignore you and just come to an understanding with it."

Miguel kept his eyes closed. He felt the prostitute's hands gently drawing back his skin and then her lips, warm and damp.

Then, somewhere down below, in his pants' pocket, his cell phone rang. They both jumped. The girl started to stand up as Miguel crouched to grab it, and he banged his cheekbone against her head. He still managed to get the phone, but his jaw was shaking so much that he couldn't say a word when he answered it.

"Daddy? Are you there, Daddy?" said Yolanda's voice.

"Yes . . . I'm here," Miguel managed to articulate.

"I wanted to know if you got the tickets. I don't trust you one bit."

"Yes, I did. Come by later and get them."

He looked at the prostitute, who had stood up and was running a hand over her head with a pained expression. He felt his cheekbone burning.

"I want to talk to you about Mom," continued Yolanda. "Do you know what she said to me last night?"

"I can't talk right now, sweetie. I've got something on the stove and it's starting to burn."

"She said that I was a moron. That I was a moron and that she was sick of me."

"I can't talk right now," repeated Miguel. "We'll discuss it when you come by."

He hung up the phone. He looked down and saw himself naked, his pants at his ankles. He backed up, dragging his feet until he hit one of the tables. He sat down on it and felt the cold touch of silverware against his butt cheek. He turned off his cell phone and placed it on the table behind him, among the plates. He brought a hand to his cheekbone. When he touched it he felt a shooting pain. The girl had come over to him and was smiling.

"Natasha . . ." Miguel started to say.

But she silenced his lips with a finger and got down on her knees again. If he hadn't felt so pathetic a second before maybe everything would have been different, but in that moment Miguel felt attacked by his own life. He was thinking that he too had a right to that, that he had the right to a little enjoyment without feeling dirty for doing it. He thought how he had an old car and a moron of a daughter and a wife he never saw anymore, and that Natasha was the only nice thing that had happened to him in years, the only unattainable thing that life had put in his reach in god knows how long: a skinny girl who ran away from secretarial school and her boyfriend to turn tricks. Miguel felt like crying, as always, but he thought that he would finally call the psychiatrist and ask her for the antidepressant.

"You have to relax a little," he heard the girl saying to him.

Then he decided to do it, and he had the strange sensation that he was giving himself something for the first time. "Maybe it'd be better if you took off your clothes, Natasha," he said.

The girl stood up immediately. She tilted her head to look at him and her hair covered her cheek, her mouth.

"You're naughty," she said. "You know that? If you want to fuck it's gonna cost you more. Fifty euros."

Miguel nodded in silence, and the girl took off her clothes as naturally as on the beach. She stood before him with her arms at her sides, so immensely fragile, so slight and so alive that Miguel had to restrain himself from hugging her. He felt a strange mix of desire and tenderness, also infinite pity for himself and for that girl who was putting a condom on him, then turning her back to him and leaning her hands on the edges of the table where she'd eaten the sandwich. Everything about her was long. A long back, cleaved by the small knolls of her vertebrae. Long, thin arms, slightly bent by angular elbows. Long legs, even longer because the girl hadn't taken off her shoes.

She held her head up, but let it drop when Miguel stood behind her. All it took was a few thrusts. The girl didn't let out a sound. Miguel a muffled groan, like a whimper from deep in his throat. Then he withdrew with a sudden feeling of horror and took off the condom. He didn't know what to do with it. Finally he left it on the plate where the sandwich had been.

He pulled up his underwear and his pants and sat in a chair. He felt deeply uneasy and his hands were trembling. He looked at the girl, who had dressed in an instant. She seemed more serious than before, as if she no longer trusted him or as if she felt uncomfortable there.

"Did you like it?" she asked.

"I don't know," answered Miguel. "I'm not feeling very well."

The girl grabbed her purse.

"Don't start getting cranky now," she said. And, after a brief pause, she added, "You have to pay me."

Miguel stood up, went into the office and grabbed five twenty-euro bills, all the ones that were there, from the register. The girl didn't comment. She folded the bills very carefully and put them in a pink coin purse.

Suddenly, as if something shook him from inside, Miguel felt the need for it not to end like that.

"Do you like music?" he asked.

She gave him a curious look.

"I have two tickets for the Apolo," said Miguel, pulling them out of his shirt pocket. "You could take your boyfriend."

The girl accepted them carefully, as if trapping a butterfly by one wing, and after a quick glance also put them away in the coin purse. Then she leaned on the counter to give Miguel a kiss on the cheek, and as she separated from him she waved the fingers on one hand. She headed toward the door and Miguel followed. He didn't know how to say good-bye to the girl, but he still felt the need to say something, something that was ordinary, that would give him the feeling that their relationship was a normal one.

"You should go to your classes," he said finally.

The girl had already reached the shutter and now turned toward him. Miguel saw her pupils electrify for an instant.

"Don't give me advice," she responded. "Nobody does, and in the end you're no different, are you? That's the way things are."

Miguel knelt down to lift the shutter. He tried to push with his legs to avoid straining his back muscles, but he still felt the pain in his side. The girl proceeded, ducking her head.

"Thanks for the sandwich," she said as she left.

Miguel lowered the shutter again. Then he discovered, beside him, the cigarette machine. He went into the office and grabbed some coins from the register. He went back to the machine. The coins burned in his hand. He began to introduce one of them into the slot. Don't do it, he said to himself.

"Don't do it," he repeated out loud, and he heard his own voice and it sounded like a plea.

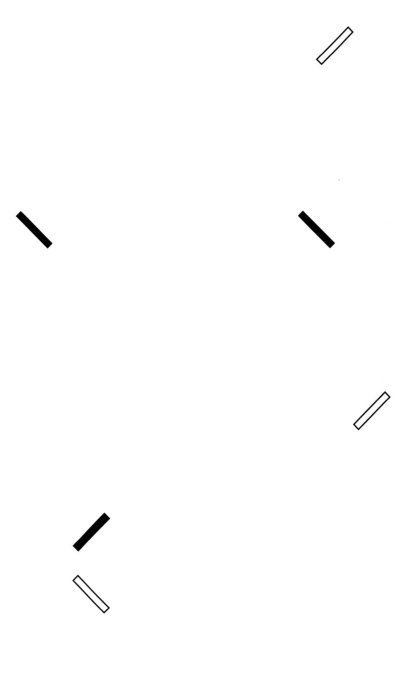

$$\textbf{Ogv} \xrightarrow[by]{trsltd} \textbf{Ch}$$

What Do You Expect, Heart

Olvido GARCÍA VALDÉS
Translated by Catherine HAMMOND

What do you expect, heart? What do you want from me?
To be like Zeno of Elea, who bit off his own tongue
in one bite
and spit it out at the tyrant?

The good angel bad
angel speaks: the bearable
the unbearable.

They look as if the quiet
captured them (a sign of danger?
how light falls at a given moment?
through a work or an internal
distillery?) in a comb of rich honey.

About what is other, I accept everything
that I do not unbearably dislike.
I accept it from the heart (who could accept
the unbearable in their heart —is that
what is unbearable—nearly inhuman?)

      What makes someone someone,
      unique, is impossible to communicate.

Some words talk
of attitude; tolerant attitude
for those who are able, the other
is tolerated. Who
are you?

The good angel bad
angel speaks: what
an ideology.

The history of women demonstrates that history
has been tolerant of women (the rung
where their lives evolved
was a rung below the rung
where the lives of the men
they depended upon evolved). Protection
soothes if it does not kill—is that love?

¿Qué esperas, corazón? ¿qué quieres de mí?
¿Y aquel, Zenón de Elea, que se cortó la lengua
de un mordisco
y se la escupió al tirano?

El ángel bueno el ángel
malo dice: lo soportable lo
insoportable.

Quedan como la quietud
las tomó (¿a una señal de peligro?
¿en un instante preciso de la caída
de la luz? ¿por un trabajo o alambique
interior?), en un panal de rica miel.

Del otro acepto todo lo que no
insoportablemente me desagrada
lo acepto de corazón (¿quién puede aceptar
de corazón lo insoportable, casi
—eso que no se soporta— inhumano?).

       Lo que hay de único y que hace de alguien alguien
       no puede ser comunicado.

Algunas palabras hablan
de la actitud; tolerante es actitud
de quien puede, el otro
es tolerado. ¿Quién
eres tú?

El ángel bueno el ángel
malo dice: qué
ideología.

La historia de las mujeres muestra que la historia
ha sido tolerante con las mujeres (el peldaño
donde se desarrollaba su vida estaba
un peldaño por debajo del peldaño
donde se desarrollaba la vida de los hombres
de quienes ellas dependían). La protección
arrulla si no mata —¿será el amor?—.

The sun dilutes us releases us and retreats
like sugar candies dissolves us not sweet
at all, in the heated sea we come undone.

> A thing must be burnt in so that it stays in the memory: only
> something that continues to hurt stays in the memory.

Crows next to sheep
their interest rests in excrement
young poplars transparent and green.

The voice of loss speaks: how strange not to hear
the voice again.

Those birds in transit,
egrets, herons, and egrets
at the bottom of the pool, the lagoon,
seemed to be angels.

> Two are better than one, because they have a good return for their
> labor: If either of them falls down, one can help the other up. Also,
> if two lie down together, they will keep warm. But how can one
> keep warm alone? Though one may be overpowered, two can
> defend themselves. A cord of three strands is not quickly broken.

Dogs prowl around
a fox, the world
opaque with thick
identifying odors.

> Do not be quick with your mouth, do not be hasty in
> your heart to utter anything before God. God is in heaven
> and you are on earth, so let your words be few.

What do you know about green, sentinel,
the green of winter, fear?
Pure firefly or sap
rise up almost without topsoil
hollow against the light.

El sol nos diluye nos destensa y repliega
como azucarillos nos disuelve nada
dulces, en el mar de calor nos deshacemos.

    Para que algo permanezca en la memoria tiene que haberse grabado
    a fuego; sólo lo que no cesa de doler permanece en la memoria.

Los grajos junto a las ovejas es
su interés el excremento verdes
transparentes alamillos.

La voz de la pérdida dice: qué raro no volver
a oír su voz.

Le parecían ángeles
aquellos pájaros en tránsito
garzas, martinetes y garzas
al pie de la charca y la laguna.

    Mejores son dos que uno; porque tienen mejor paga de su
    trabajo. Porque si cayeren, el uno levantará a su compañero. También
    si dos durmieren juntos, se calentarán; mas ¿cómo se calentará uno
    solo? Y si alguno prevaleciere contra el uno, dos estarán
    contra él; y cordón de tres dobleces no presto se rompe.

Perros merodean cerca
de un zorro, opaco
el mundo en su espesor
olores que identifican.

    No te des prisa con tu boca, ni tu corazón se apresure
    a proferir palabra delante de Dios; porque Dios está en el cielo,
    y tú sobre la tierra: por tanto, sean pocas tus palabras.

¿Qué sabes de lo verde, centinela,
verde de invierno, miedo?
Sin casi mantillo brota
pura luciérnaga o savia
hueco trasluz.

[1] Con la incorporación de fragmentos de Décio Pignatari, Nietzsche y el Ecclesiastés.

$$Mp \xrightarrow[by]{trsltd} Mt$$

Under the Sign of Anaximander

Miquel DE PALOL
Translated by Martha TENNENT

I

I was raised by a depressed mother and an alcoholic father. Mother soon stopped being a mom in every sense of the word and became more of a nuisance than an iconic figure, just a body to trip over. And Pops was tripping on her less and less, 'cause when my older sisters seemed ready, straight away he started banging them, first one then the other, till finally he was banging one in front of the other, and I was starting to see myself as next on the list; soon as the girls started holding off, or skipped town, or were simply bored, the next ruptured hole was going to be my ass. And my old lady was present through it all, with her ashen skin and vacant look.

One afternoon when I came home from school I encountered a most unusual spectacle. The next-door neighbor had Mom against the kitchen table and was fucking her to the tick-tock rhythm of a clock, the creaking of the table legs marking the tempo. Neither of them seemed bothered by my presence, nothing changed, Mom, gripping the sides of the table with her hands, same face as always, a perfect void, emptied of desire and opinions. They hadn't even taken their clothes off. Mom, her skirt rolled up to her waist, the neighbor's trousers crumpled on the floor around his shoes like an enormous, dark water lily, at the base of those skinny, hairy white legs, trembling and offensive. The bottom of his shirt was flapping against his ass: this was the point of greatest movement. I put down my folder and pencil case and walked over to the kitchen cupboard and took out some crackers, trying my best not to attract attention, but then I wasn't particularly worried about hiding my presence either; I grabbed a glass, made my way to the fridge in search of milk, and filled it.

I started munching as I looked out the window onto the courtyard, looking without seeing, without thinking, no particular feeling that I could articulate or identify. I couldn't tell you how long I'd stood there, probably not as long as it seemed, when I jerked around as the front door opened with that familiar intensity. Dad entered and came to a halt a meter from Mom and the neighbor, all three petrified, sort of like they were frozen in some photograph. Then, all at the same time, like they'd just heard the starter's pistol, one was yanking his trousers up, the other rummaging in a drawer, and Mom—slowly standing up, turning around without changing expression, like she was from some other world—let her skirt fall, fatality drawing it downward to a more presentable position.

Dad had grabbed the largest knife in the drawer before the neighbor was zipped up, and in the perfect silence of the room, he stabbed him forty-eight times, all over his body, methodical, thorough, conscientious. He let him drop in the middle of the room, and when the guy had stopped moving, no jerks, no residual movements, Dad stood there staring at him, like he was contemplating a job well done; then he scrubbed his hands and all the way up to his elbows, cleaned the knife with the green sponge, dried it, and put it back in the drawer. Mom's expression never changed. Dad turned to me:

"Listen," he said calmly, speaking slowly. "Now I'm going to tell you, down to the last detail, how we're going to explain this. Pay attention, 'cause they're going to ask us over and over, and there can't be no changes, no hesitation."

First off, he presented the whole story in an orderly fashion, next, how we should respond if they asked this, how if they asked that; and all the while Mom was rubbing up against the edge of the table, one leg lifted, then against the arm of the rocking chair, same rhythm as before, against the knob on the stove, anything would do the trick as long as it was hard, smooth, steady, and handy, same expression on her face, and the neighbor just laying there, blending into the floor, in a position that struck me as pretty dynamic, but the longer I stared, the more definitive it seemed, a puddle of blood forming slowly, steadily on the right side of the body that increasingly resembled the west coast of the island of England.

I told them everything the way Dad said to, made no mistakes in any of the subsequent interrogations, but they still threw him in the can, and Mom was sent to a state mental institution for the destitute, the older sister went to work at the Fabre & Coats factory, the younger to live with Grandma in Norfolk, and me, the judge put me in foster care, but I got out of there soon as I could and found a living down at the docks.

II

The way of life I'd learned from Pops proved most helpful. On more than one occasion, finding myself in an extremely difficult situation, I'd stop to think: now what would Dad do here? And that not only saved my life but purveyed me material benefits. I'm not talking about doing what the old man would have done, but rather the opposite. Dad would've done that, so I'll do this. I was barely twenty years old and had already managed to achieve a remarkable position in life, and what's more important, I was respected among the wholesale distributors, even though I didn't have a degree Once a year, more or less, my younger sister would send news about the family, nothing to lose any sleep over. Dad was still behind bars and big sister had become a hooker, though she passed herself off as a tour guide.

One day I learned that Mom had died, and I had the strangest feeling. And I was informed that Dad had served more than a third of his sentence, and every other week now he got out 'cause of good behavior. I kept my eyes peeled, trailed him, and when, just like I suspected, he went for a night hunt, I waited for him in a clearing, in the darkest spot, and shot him five times, the last right between the eyes.

That same night I went hunting for my older sister and didn't tell her who I was till I'd fucked her. At first she didn't believe me, but when I furnished sufficient evidence, details, impossible-to-invent anecdotes, when I responded to all her questions, even though I wasn't much inclined to, then she cursed me, tried to belt me, so I left, but not before making sure I'd put her out of work for a while.

The very next day, I visited my younger sister—Grandma had died and the house was now hers—and gave her the rundown. She appeared confounded, incapable of reacting, so I had to take matters into my own hands; I did her four times and beat the crap out of her. Justice had been done. But by shouldering the misery of the world, I had also acquired a substantial obligation. I had become the Exterminating Angel, and in order to restore peace to myself, I had no choice but to incarnate absolute goodness from then on.

The following day the members of the Central Commission of the Waterfront Cooperative held an important event. A committee from the House of Commons had organized a meeting to discuss needs and conditions for expanding the shipyard and building a new breakwater, and so us long-time rakes all donned our best suits and flashiest ties for the occasion.

The meeting was smooth sailing, and afterward we invited the committee to dine at the Co-op's terrace restaurant. We were all standing around, stiff with cold, having a cocktail, when a couple MPs introduced their wives to us. When I shook the hand of the juiciest dame, I turned to her husband and said:

"Ah, shit, so this pork chop is your little missus?" An icy silence followed, and having achieved my moment of glory, I topped it off, "She any good with BJs? Doesn't look like she would be, with that asshole of a mouth." I grabbed one of her tits, she shrank back, I advanced. "You could always try wanking on this. Shall we give it a stab?"

Three of the thumbscrew boys dragged me outside.

"What's got into you?" shouted my mentor, the head honcho at the Commission, on the front porch of the restaurant. "You off your rocker?"

"Just the opposite, I'm simply recalibrating the scales of justice."

"What the hell are you babbling about? Trying to sink the whole deal?"

"Nothing could be farther from my intention. I'm searching for profundities."

"And how are you planning to go about this, if I might ask?" he shot back. (I made a gesture that said: wait and see.) "Go back in there and apologize to the man, tell him you're going through a rough spell and the drink went to your head."

"There ain't no rough spell and I'm not drunk."

He turned to his thugs.

"Take him out to the pantry and see that when you're done with him he's left without a social life for a week." We were out of sight when he yelled: "But don't overdo it, boys."

III

Nothing could be more reactionary than compartmentalized behavior: here I have to behave like a gentleman, there like a pig. It's the worst possible show of contempt, cowardice, and meanness, one more aspect of the moral exercise of public virtues and private vices. Well no: pariahs deserve considerably more respect than princes, sluts more than ladies. That and many other profound thoughts occupied my brain at that moment; I'd have been able to think more and much clearer had I not been tethered to the radiator in the laundry room in the head office of the Commission, unable to dry the blood dripping down my nose and cheek, mixing with my snot, and I didn't know how many broken bones I had; Anaximander said it himself—though I didn't even know he existed at the time—that things have a way of canceling each other out, debts and compensations, according to the judgment of Time. Among the pariahs I would behave like a monk, among the monks like a criminal.

I knew what was coming, and I shuddered to consider the angles at which the blows would land. But I got off pretty easy: a few more punches to the stomach, the usual detailed proviso of warnings and threats, a string of forbidden conduct, folks I needed to avoid for the rest of my life—and me back on the street with my tail between my legs. I was feeling kind of low and in my moment of consternation decided to visit the sisters to ask for their forgiveness, and, you know, just in case, see if I could get some dough out of them. The older had the Swedish truck driver she lived with throw me down the stairs, the younger—who wasn't so young now, and had become a bodybuilder, or something along that line, anyway stronger that me who wasn't eating much those days—well, she threw me down the stairs herself.

I didn't know what I wanted or what I should do, not even what my options were—the possibilities within myself, in my environment, my own aptitudes—but it all seemed to be leading me to a turning point in which my transience might easily develop into the paralyzing dependence typical of an addict. I had personally explored my father's territory, had even killed his physical body, and I bundled up what I'd gained from the experience and stuck it up my ass, but none of it served to free me of my original debt. I realized that nothing had happened just because, but rather I had been chosen to bear the sins of the world, and whether or not the world liked it or not or would merely sit back and watch me with indifference, none of that affected my resolve. I abandoned my country, crossed the ocean, lived in foreign lands, devoted myself to grotesque jobs, even had the fantasy once that I'd return, just for the inane reason that I'd have to leave again. And I ended up being carried away by the supreme illusion: the rarefied quietude of the Mediterranean shores.

IV

One day I spotted huge headlines in the newspapers announcing a car bombing in the parking lot of the central bus station, and the black lettering was so attractive that I knew immediately, without hesitation, what I should do. I headed straight for the General Directorate of Security and asked to see the chief. I was referred to a subordinate, but soon as they heard my story I was arrested, moved to another room, videotaped, and some seven or eight guys came to listen to me, the chief himself present all the while.

"Start over," the first guy grumbled at me.

"It was me."

"You what?"

"I planted the bomb at the station."

They introduced me to a public defender, made me repeat my story ten or twelve times, they entered and left in pairs, who knows how many times, whispered to each other, and there I was so conscious that from a world perspective—judged according to the scales of the World—I had committed the crime (that crime and a thousand others) that I seriously considered grabbing one of the cops' guns and emptying the clip till they finally shot me down. In the end, they left me alone with my lawyer, who spoke these words:

"Sorry, but based on your story—I can't imagine what could have possessed you to behave thus—it's impossible for you to have done it. Nevertheless, since they don't have anything else on you, they're willing to charge you with obstruction of justice and contempt of authority. I've insisted that you undergo a psychological evaluation, and according to the results, you'll probably be set free with the obligation to follow the prescribed treatment."

"My head's in fine condition, "I told him. "I don't need no psychiatric treatment."

"You prefer to go to jail?"

He struck me as a reasonable guy and I opted to tell the truth.

"There's an imbalance of hierophantic forces that I aim to set right. So, this means that even if I didn't commit the crime in material terms, it was in fact me."

We held each other in a steady poker gaze.

"Don't worry," he told me with a smile of complicity, "I know just the person you should speak to."

Everything went exactly like the public defender had foreseen, and soon I realized that I wasn't the least bit innocent. They ran two different tests, one ordered by the prosecution, the other by my lawyer, and they discovered that I suffered from a mild bipolar disorder; I was treated as an outpatient under strict medical and police control, with various obligations to show up here and there every week. And I was free.

Not fifteen days had elapsed when the public defender—a fellow by the name of Ariman—called me in. I went thinking there was some complication in my case, but soon as I entered his office (and, incidentally, he made me wait quite a while) I found him accompanied by some other guy—an old man, tall and thin—I don't know how to communicate the impression he made on me, both thin and corpulent at the same time, like some kind of derelict ghost of a man but at the same time indestructible, and this guy shot me such a tough look that I averted my eyes. The lawyer had me sit down and not only did he not bother to introduce me, but he started talking like I wasn't even present.

"Could it be that he simply pretended—and so clumsily—to commit the crime to disguise the fact that he actually did it?" the old man asked. To which my lawyer replied:

"Following that line of reasoning, why would he have turned himself in, if there wasn't any evidence linking him to the scene?"

They must have been attempting to involve me in the crime or testing me, and I had the distinct impression that what I did or failed to do in the next five minutes would determine the rest of my life.

"Excuse me," I interrupted, "If you're referring to me, there's no need to waste any more of your time on speculations. I planted the bomb, and whether you believe me or not is of no consequence."

"But, then of course," the old man said, hardly glancing at me, "not believing him might provide him the reason he needs to continue thus."

"Excuse me, Sir, "I said, appealing to the old man, wondering if it was worth the trouble to be polite, "but I believe that I'm at a disadvantage here."

"Just be patient, Curdwyn," my lawyer said, "Don't worry, you'll have it your way and you'll even come out ahead. For now, you don't need to know the name of your benefactor. (I deduced he was referring to the old man, but I didn't know what I had benefited from.) For the sake of convenience, however, you can address him as Mister Swann."

I feigned an attack of courtesy.

"I'm very pleased to make your acquaintance, Mister Swann."

I was suffused with a sense of infinite patience as I awaited my chance.

V

I paid close attention to the news during the following days, and I didn't have to wait long. One weekend there was an attempt on the Prime Minister, and I raced to the Police Station to claim my part in it. At first I assembled a group of policemen who didn't know me and were very attentive, to such a degree that for a moment I was sure they were going to rough me up. But then the big bosses appeared, and soon as they spotted me their expressions turned to scowls of disgust and disappointment.

"You got nothing else to do?" asked the officer who had taken my statement the first time. He was starting to feel like family.

I demanded to be heard, disclosed all sorts of details about my scheme. But when they asked for the names of my accomplices, I blew the whole thing by hesitating. We all know that hesitation is never neutral territory, and apparently practice makes it easier to distinguish between someone who hesitates because he's reluctant to divulge what he doesn't want to, someone who actually doesn't know what he's talking about, and the guy who's just putting on an act. Who knows, maybe they were trying to set me up, and when I realized it, it was too late, I wasn't in time to feign improvisation—which for that matter would have been pretty close to the truth—but the disappointed face gave me away.

Nevertheless, I reeled off some names, which at the time seemed an irresistible mixture, but now it strikes me as rather tame: common criminals, top members of armed gangs, international terrorists, bankers who had absconded—I even interpolated invented names here and there. They laughed as they listened.

"Good day, Sir," snapped the officer from the first meeting. "Do us a favor would you, don't waste any more of our time."

Things were looking bad. No legal proceedings, no charges, nothing this time around. I considered the possibility of actually committing a crime of considerable social consequences. It wasn't enough to sit back and wait for it, knowing that the appropriate crime would eventually be committed—it and others—especially since no one was better equipped than me to atone for it, and with such neatness and distinction, so completely. Something else was needed. The expiatory path to goodness is tortuous and full of thorns! Tears of gratitude are so difficult to obtain and so very dear!

VI

In five months I pleaded guilty to one kidnapping, another bombing, the assassination of a traffic officer, and one mass poisoning (the authorship of which was later claimed by a small group called The Liberation Sect). The police insisted that my lawyer keep me under control, something exceedingly difficult within the letter and spirit of the law, but Ariman did what he could. One day he invited me to lunch in a posh restaurant, and just like I thought, he was accompanied by the enigmatic Mr. Swann.

"Curdwyn," my lawyers says to me, "we can't keep this up any longer. It's time for you to tell us what's going on in that head of yours. You've been very skillful and you have no criminal record, but we do know that a few years ago you were part of an organization engaged in illegal trade in the U.K. That's why your present attitude proves more complex and at the same time less clear. You must stop trying to atone for the sins of the world. You're moved by Goodness, I know, but not everyone is in a position to appreciate this."

"What can I say? Until my debt is paid off, I can't do otherwise. And I can't do this except in absolute terms."

"What absolute terms?" Swann asked. "Good and Evil are not hierarchical categories, but rather degrees of the same substance, and as predicates they blend together, like black and white (which aren't substances either) to form figures that are grey or some other color, where one or the other predominates. Rarely can one be found in a pure state, unless someone has worked diligently in the distilling process."

"Evil's the black one, right? And Good, the white?"

"No, it's just the opposite," Swann said, but I was sure he was improvising.

"And so?" I said with a touch of impatience. "How does this translate into what I'm supposed to do?"

"It's more what you shouldn't do," said Ariman. "Mister Swann and I are worried about what you might be capable of doing."

Swann observed me, as an entomologist might a specimen.

"Let's see if I've understood this correctly." I said. "If I'm moved by Evil, I shouldn't neglect the presence of Good, but if I'm moved by Good, I shouldn't neglect Evil."

"The problem lies with the adversative," Ariman said. "The order in which you phrased your sentence suggests a hierarchy of dangerous values."

"You're worried that I might have committed some of the crimes I lay claim to?" I said. They didn't utter a word. "Or maybe you think that I didn't carry them out and I'm going loco-bonkers." More silence. "Maybe you're worried, according to this value system, that I might commit them and you'll find yourselves involved."

Swann shot me a military look, one of piercing symmetry.

"Your lawyer is almost as kind as you are yourself, but if you'll forgive me, I'm not a sentimental type nor do I have time to be one."

"So, you want me to certify, Sir, that I can claim to be author of any crimes I wish," I said interrupting the gentleman, not daring to address him with a show of familiarity, "as long as I don't commit them."

Swann stepped away, glanced into the distance then back at me, and I had the impression that his eyes were more intent in their fixity that he saw deeper inside me than ever before. I found it hard to imagine the tender child this terrible old man had once been.

"On the contrary," he said slowly but not with a serious tone—it was almost an offhand remark. "If you claim authorship of another crime, I want you to guarantee that you have actually committed the crime."

I waited for them to laugh, explain the joke, but like a couple of automatons they simply turned and looked at me. I was really discombobulated now; they had made me backtrack on my road to Damascus and the rectitude I had resolved upon.

VII

I found myself wondering if I would suddenly discover some meaning to that which has none and never will. What exactly is the difference between a real solution and an invented one?

"Mister Swann," I said, "I understand that in one way or another I am on the point of rendering you an important service."

"Excellent, Curdwyn, from the very beginning it was clear that you were no fool. You want to know what your prospects will be once this is over."

"More or less, Mister Swann. I would like to know."

"And what exactly do you know how to do?" Ariman asked, and the two of them chuckled. "Because of course, though it may not be an important detail, it should be taken into account."

It didn't strike me that a display of my skills was a good way to further my options.

Swann spoke with a professorial tone:

"With God dead, His attributes have been hacked into pieces and distributed among us in this carnage of existence. Performance: media stars. Power: bankers. Being in itself: Art. Where among these would you say that you fit?"

I pretended to be buried in deepest thought.

"In Art, maybe?"

They burst into laughter. "I told you so. Another total waste."

$$\mathbf{CAm} \xrightarrow[\text{by}]{\text{trsltd}} \mathbf{Fm}$$

Crossing Bridges

César Antonio MOLINA
Translated by Francisco MACÍAS

I crossed the Vltava by way of the Charles Bridge.
I crossed the Neva by way of the Trinity Bridge.
I crossed the Danube by way of the Lion Bridge.
I crossed the Moskva by way of the Novoarbatski Bridge.
I crossed the Sava by way of Branko's Bridge.
I crossed the Tiber by way of the ponte Sant'Angelo.
I crossed the Seine by way of the pont Mirabeau.
I crossed the bridges of rusted iron over the immense Paraná,
at Gualeguaychú,
and the equally mighty Santa Lucía River
at the entryway of old Montevideo.
And now I am traversing the East River
by way of the Brooklyn Bridge.
Which one of them will be the bridge of my dreams?
I am immobile in the air halfway between
Manhattan and Brooklyn. The East River at my feet:
dense, uninhabited, without flowing. So is my blood.
And a bit of a breeze lifting the skirts of the schoolgirls.
Halfway there like the navel of that young woman,
halfway there between the shrunken T-shirt
and the beginning of her marked pubis due to the sagging pants.
Thus I am in the middle of the bridge of Brooklyn,
In the midst of all the bridges of the world.
The noble neo-gothic arches of Manhattan bidding me farewell,
those of Brooklyn awaiting me.
This middle of the road, this power to choose
between continuing or returning, this no-man's-land
in the middle of the air is, like Whitman wrote,
the best medicine for the soul.
Isn't the soul also something aerial?
Seated on this bench, in the middle of the bridge,
the jam stops a large black limousine
 right between the interstices of the woodwork.
It moves toward Brooklyn but it returns to Manhattan
And so on and so forth.
Here I feel how the axis of my life becomes displaced
from the past unto the present and the four eyes
of the arches conceive my future.
The towers of the bridge, on either side,
despite the fog, they are clearly
defined. They are the twin sisters of the other giants.
Am I daydreaming? Or, more precisely, am I waking from a dream?

Crucé el Moldava por el puente de Carlos.
Crucé el Neva por el puente de la Trinidad.
Crucé el Danubio por el puente de los Leones.
Crucé el Moscova por el puente Novoarbatski.
Crucé el Sava por el puente de Branko.
Crucé el Tíber por el ponte Sant´Angelo.
Crucé el Sena por el puente Mirabeau.
Crucé los puentes de hierro oxidado sobre el inmenso Paraná,
en Gualeguaychu,
y el no menos caudaloso río Santa Lucía
a la entrada del antiguo Montevideo.
Y ahora estoy atravesando el East River
por el puente de Brooklyn.
¿Cuál de ellos será el puente de mis sueños?
Estoy inmóvil en el aire a mitad de camino entre
Manhattan y Brooklyn. El East River a mis pies:
denso, deshabitado, sin fluir. Así mi sangre.
Y una poca brisa levantando las faldas de las escolares.
A mitad de camino como el ombligo de aquella joven,
a mitad de camino entre la camiseta encogida
y el comienzo de su pubis marcado por el caído pantalón.
Así estoy yo en medio del puente de Brooklyn,
en medio de todos los puentes del mundo.
Los nobles arcos neogóticos de Manhattan despidiéndome,
esperándome los de Brooklyn.
Esta mitad del camino, este poder elegir
entre continuar o regresar, esta tierra de nadie
en medio del aire es, como escribió Whitman,
la mejor medicina para el alma.
¿No es el alma también algo aéreo?
Sentado en este banco, en medio del puente,
el atasco detiene a una gran limusina negra
justo entre los intersticios del maderamen.
Va hacia Brooklyn pero regresa a Manhattan
y así sucesivamente.
Aquí siento cómo el eje de mi vida se desplaza
desde el pasado al presente y los cuatro ojos
de los arcos conciben mi futuro.
Las torres del puente, a uno y otro lado,
a pesar de la neblina, están claramente
definidas. Son hermanas gemelas de los otros gigantes.
¿Sueño despierto o, más bien, despierto del sueño?

I am halfway there and I linger.
My friends take a seat by me,
meanwhile someone takes a photo of us that is veiled
by a cyclist who passes without stopping.
Sorry!
Sorry!
She cries raising her arms from the handlebar.
At least something remained etched in us
of her fresh face.
I cross bridges just as storms.
What side will they cast us?
I seek repose in all things.
All of whom passed I met when
I was under the leaves of the fig tree.
When I am weak, then I am strong,
my strength is powerful in weakness.
I cross bridges just as I leave dreams in hotels.
And through the towpaths flow impassive rivers.
Seated upon the bench I remain in silence.
The silence belongs to the art of oratory.
It rains over the Paraná.
It snows over the Neva.
My gaze is so innocent that it deceives.

Estoy a mitad del camino y remoloneo.
Mis amigos toman asiento junto a mí,
mientras uno nos hace una foto que es velada
por una ciclista que pasa sin detenerse.
¡Sorry!
¡Sorry!
grita levantando los brazos del manillar.
Al menos se quedó en nosotros algo impreso
de su fresco rostro.
Cruzo puentes como tormentas.
¿A qué lado nos echarán?
Busco reposo en todas las cosas.
A cuantos pasan los conocí cuando
estaba bajo las hojas de la higuera.
Cuando soy débil, entonces soy fuerte,
mi fuerza es poderosa en las debilidades.
Cruzo puentes como dejo sueños en los hoteles.
Y por los caminos de sirga fluyen ríos impasibles.
Sentado sobre el banco permanezco en silencio.
El silencio pertenece al arte de la oratoria.
Llueve sobre el Paraná.
Nieva sobre el Neva.
Mi mirada es tan inocente que engaña.

$$\textbf{CAm} \xrightarrow[by]{trsltd} \textbf{Fm}$$

Bitter Lemons

César Antonio MOLINA
Translated by Francisco MACÍAS

Everything went well until we got to Corfu. It's not that things started to go wrong there, but what happened there may have been an omen that our happiness had already been drawn out far too long. I was a new professor. Upon completing my first course as a lecturer, I bought myself a car: a white Fiat 127. My goal was to travel through Greece that summer, traversing those historic and literary places of which I had dreamed since my childhood. I was neither financially nor physically able to do this alone; and all the promises made to accompany me had fallen through.

Time was short; and it occurred to me to post a flyer in the faculty area. Two female students confirmed their interest with a phone call. I had had them in my course, but that relationship had ended. I set out with Maite and Victoria, from whom I was separated by only a few years. At first, it felt odd to travel with the girls after I had maintained a certain degree of professional distance from them; but their good nature and humor brought us closer very soon. We all drove; we all liked the monuments and ruins and the camaraderie, which reduced the effects of the heat and our exhaustion. We had made our way across the south of France and then Italy; and we were already in the Brindisi-to-Corfu ferry to cross onto the mainland. I announced our arrival at the port, and upon seeing the buildings that welcomed us there, I couldn't discern a difference from one country to another. Pompous Mussolinian constructions gave way to

buildings and plazas, imported from the ancient French and English metropo-
lises, in the historic center of the capital. It was dawn; we had the whole day
ahead of us, and we decided to find a more rustic seaside place, removed from
the hustle and bustle of the city. The road signs took us to the northwest of the island. We were on the coastal road. We passed through Alykes, Kontokali, and the
majestic Venetian shipyards of Gouvia, then Kommeno, Daphnila, and, finally,
Dassia, which had an immense beach nearly fifteen kilometers long. Orchards
reached down to the whitest sands. There, in the Ionian Sea, we were able to take
our first Greek bath. I lay down under the shade of some olive trees, and when
I woke up, I saw Victoria still floating on the water and Maite, who returned
from who knows where, gesticulating with an elderly woman all dressed in
black. She had found, in that very spot, lodging. It was an old stable, which was
now coarsely renovated. It had three bunks, a dining table, and a small oven, all
in one open space. Outside were the water closet and a washbasin that served as
both a bath and shower without hot water. The price was reasonable, and the
small barrack seemed a suitable place to gain new strength for the assault on
the Greek mainland. The landlady's house and grove were very close, and the
woman would gather fresh fruit and vegetables for us. All was perfect, even in
the intimate chastity that we practiced. Time passed slowly and I allowed myself
to get lost in the "why?" of earthly things, while they became brackish women,
iodized and with aquatic eyes, with seaweed hair that was tousled by the nets
that were hanging from the ceiling like bridal veils. From our encampment we
went up to the north of the island, to Kassiopi, where Tiberius built another
one of his mansions, and we also headed down toward the south. At Gastouri
was the Achilleion, a palace built by Sisi, the melancholic empress, in honor of
Thetis and Achilles—a neoclassical building, with beautiful gardens headed by
the statues of the triumphant hero, fatally wounded in the heel. At Korkyra we
spent many afternoons in the terraces of the Spianada Square, which reminded
us of the Rue de Rivoli of Paris. While they frugally window-shopped the narrow streets, I visited the sculpture of Medusa, she who mortally enthralled. Her
demented smile, her bulging eyes, the curly snakes of her hair and her waist,
her immense mouth from which a wide and bifurcated tongue must have stuck
out like that of a snake, they petrified me. I felt well in the island of the Phaea-
cians, where Nausicaa found the wayward Ulysses; but the days proposed for
the last stop had passed. I kept reminding them of an imminent departure that
never happened. At every daybreak, I was hidden by them in the dense down of
their pubis. I came to understand that I was sweetly anchored when I confirmed
that both young women had suspended their depilatory practices and that their
bodies ran freely under their flimsy clothes. I gazed upon them as they slept,
homely and enigmatic, and the hour to leave escaped me. The bedroom became
covered with scattered objects; the clothes were stirred in disarray. I enjoyed
being one more object. I didn't brush away the dust that began to cover them.

Everything remained where it was, in the same manner and arrangement. I was entangled in their clothes, and I didn't feel the nostalgia of my domestic order. In that place I could not even manage to put myself in order. I remained enveloped by all those forms that were scattered by the clouds across that firmament and also within my heart.

The car was perfectly prepared to continue the trip and my suitcase ready. Yet I inspected an old bicycle, oiled its chain, and set out at dawn, slowly, to walk along the shoreline. I managed to reach Ipsos—a sandlot covered with pebbles—and climbed Mount Pantokrator, the highest mountain of the island, surrounded by forests and overlooking the bay. On this morning stroll I came across the ferries that arrived from Italy or those that set out en route to Patras. At the end of the sandlot that was Dassia, along a curve from which you could no longer see the spot we'd set out from, there was a beverage stand that served drinks all night as if it were a bustling nightclub. Upon one of its walls was its name: *"La tortuga ecuestre"* [The Equestrian Turtle]. A bit earlier, at a safe distance from that playful outdoor locale, I watched as a couple of large trucks took their place. They carried the lighting equipment and props for a film shoot. I stopped in my tracks and looked for a good perspective from which I could get distracted by the work of others. Little by little, from the depths of those great stomachs, emerged the spotlights, cranes, rails, and cameras, along with the cables and other objects that were unknown to me. At the end, due to the familiarity that shared time grants us, I learned about this equipment from one of the laborers who shot outdoor footage for a movie set on the island. To ensure my solitude, I shared nothing with my captors. I decided to return the next day and offer my services here, even if for free. I woke up at first light and left them in their slumber, abandoning them in their undressed geography. Sometimes I would lie back on the cot and gaze upon them until they woke, not to get lost in desire but to keep watch over their dreams. Maite's hair was denser than Victoria's, but the latter's took root in more abyssal zones.

When I arrived at the set preparation was already underway. By now those first few trucks had been hitched to other trailers to shelter some of the actors and the director himself. My voluntary help served to haul the heavy loads and to better prepare everything. But my research on the information sheet for the film did not progress much. I was able to deduce from the comments made that it was a *peplum* [sword-and-sandal], and this brought on a very special surge of excitement, to find myself in Greece and to attend the filming of a cinematographic genre so dear to me. As the day progressed, that strange landscape of scattered objects became covered with actors in period costumes. I understood immediately, based on their attire, that they were not Romans but Greeks, and this first requirement came to be confirmed by the slate blackboard where the following title was written in Italian: *I rostri di Helena* [The Rostra of Helen]. If I had not developed a sort of friendship with the technicians and agreed to lend a helping hand, I would have returned to my restless and contemplative state, for I discovered how boring, slow, and tedious it is to make a film. The end of the work day was resolved with nothing but a few minutes of suitable celluloid. On the sixth day of being engaged in these matters, awaiting my friends' latest promises to leave, I arrived at the film shoot, as always, at the break of dawn. Concerns and expectations were higher, because that day would not involve extras or supporting actors but the main protagonists. Everything seemed ready and, even then, three hours had to pass in order for the action to resume. I was seated in the shadow of a giraffe sipping a soft drink, when I heard the door to one of those mobile dressing rooms. Out came Helen who, to my surprise, was none other than the actress Rossana Podestà, who had already played the same role, some ten years ago, in Robert Wise's film Helen of Troy. The scene being shot was being interpreted by three actors, two men and a woman, surrounded by a small army corps, in the middle of the beach. One of them tried to pierce Helen with a sword, while the other warrior blocked the weapon. Among the three, a dialog of threats and accusations developed that ended with the forgiveness of the protagonist. Several scenes were reshot not because of errors or flaws in diction or gestures, but because the actor who played the threatening role did it with such violence; so much so that he exceeded the demands of the director's instructions. During lunch I learned that the dispute would re-enact Agamemnon's quarrel with his brother Menelaus, in which he tries to prevent the latter from killing his treacherous wife. And that extreme violence, exacerbated by incessant repetition, stemmed from the ongoing conflicts of the protagonist couple, who had recently split up in real life. The interiors of this Italo-Franco-German coproduction had already been shot in the Cineccità studios in Rome. The film attempted to recreate what might have happened to this woman "rich in men," after the fall and burning of Troy. For that purpose, the screenwriter and director, Duccio de Martino, borrowed from three different stories, told by Euripides, Hesiod, and Virgil in antiquity. The first scene, as in *The Trojan Women*, depicted a tragic woman, suicidal, making sacrifices in order to wash away the guilt that had provoked such a disgraceful series of events. However, Hesiod exonerated her of any responsibility given that she had never been in Troy and her recollection was nothing but a false, supplanted, image. As for Virgil, in the *Æneid*, he made Venus stay Aeneas's sword from piercing her as punishment for her treason to the Trojans and the delivery of her defenseless brother-in-law, Deiphobus, to the fierce vengeance of Menelaus. They had chosen Corfu to film the outdoor scenes due to its proximity, isolation, the economy, and variety of the scenery. Rossana spent most of her time alone, since no one wanted to take a side one way or another, with respect to the private quarrel. At the end of the day, that mythical Helen climbed into her sports car and disappeared to the hotel.

When I returned to our lodging and told Maite and Victoria about my little adventure, they showed a certain amount of jealousy and announced —after weeks of delay—their willingness to leave the island and resume our interrupted journey. I refused and told them—a white lie—of my commitment to the production to work until the end of filming, in a couple of weeks. My real intention was to see, face to face, that new Helen of flesh and bone and, above all, to touch her hands. In *Helen of Troy*, Rossana Podestà played the role of a faithful woman in love; Jacques Sernas portrayed Paris. When he dies at the hands of Menelaus, in the midst of the burning and pillaging of the city, after the entry of Ulysses's wooden horse, she holds him, and her white tunic and her hands end up covered in blood. In the following scene, the last one, Helen is on a ship headed back for Greece. Menelaus still sees her bloodstained clothes and grasps her wrists to look at her hands. Then, with great ire, he orders her to change and to wash up. And she, staring with hate, answers: "Never!"

The exterior shots changed to places not far from that first location. I kept watch for the moment of our encounter. Because of my position of constant watch, I could see how Steve Reeves, leaving the company of Stanley Baker and Cedric Hardwicke, made his way toward Rossana when she retired from the set to her dressing room trailer. He stopped her and they exchanged a few words. She rejected him, and he grabbed her in a furious manner and threw her to the floor. I sprang to her aid and received a hard blow to the head, inflicted with the same Achaean helmet he held in his hands. For a few minutes, I lost consciousness. When I came to, my whole face was soaked in blood and the gash opened in my brow was still bleeding. Next to me was Rossana, or who knows, Helen, with her *peplum* and her hands stained with my blood trying to contain the violent hemorrhage.

Maite and Victoria welcomed me like abandoned lovers, a role I had never played. We spoke of our departure—we had been there nearly two months; and, again, it was impossible for us to come to an agreement. They insisted on spending September there, too. But my time was running out, and I felt I should no longer roam the Greek mainland but return to Madrid for September exams. I loaded my Fiat 127, and on the next day, when I turned the ignition, I saw that it didn't work. For several days, I was subjected to their ruses, which were, indeed, pleasant and witty. On September 14, the date of my birthday, I took them to celebrate at *La tortuga ecuestre*. They drank and danced to exhaustion while I feigned the same. I struggled to make them return and they fell exhausted on their cots. I saw them for the last time, undressed and unwary. Then, for some unknown reason, I took a safety razor from one of their toiletry kits, and gingerly shaved the down from their pubis which I saved in a book of its own, as with dry leaves.

From the stern of the ferry that was heading for Brindisi, I saw the shadow of the hills over the fields of wheat, the vineyards, the olive trees, the orange trees, and the bitter lemon trees of the island.

Contributors

/

/Fernando ARAMBURU

Fernando Aramburu was born in San Sebastian in 1959. He was a founding member of CLOC, a group of Art and DisArt that combined countercultural expression with the practice of surrealistic humor. He was a staff writer for the literary magazine *KANTIL*. He earned a degree in Hispanic language and literature at the University of Zaragoza. He has lived in the Federal Republic of Germany since 1985, dedicated entirely to his writing after having spent years as a teacher. His literary career began with poetry, which was published in a nearly complete volume in 1993 by the University of the Basque Country under the title *Bruma y conciencia*, a partially bilingual edition in Spanish and Euskera. Another book of poems was compiled some years later under the title *Yo quisiera llover* (2010).

His first novel, *Fuegos con limón*, was published in 1996, followed by *Los ojos vacíos* (Euskadi Prize 2001), *El trompetista del Utopía, Vida de un piojo llamado Matías, Bami sin sombre, Viaje con Clara por Alemania*, and *Años lentos* (Tusquets Prize, 2011). Includes short prose: *El artista y su cadáver,* and the short-story collections: *No ser no duele, Los peces de la amargura* (Prize of the Spanish Royal Academy, 2008) and *El vigilante del fiordo*. He has also written for children and has worked translating German authors into Spanish. He contributes often to literary supplements and his work has been translated into many languages.

Willis BARNSTONE\

Willis Barnstone, born in Lewiston, Maine, and educated at Bowdoin, the Sorbonne, SOAS, Columbia, and Yale, taught in Greece at the end of the civil war (1949–51), and in Buenos Aires during the Dirty War. During the Cultural Revolution he went to China, where he was later a Fulbright Professor at Beijing Foreign Studies University (1984–1985). Former O'Connor Professor of Greek at Colgate University, he is Distinguished Professor Emeritus of Comparative Literature and Spanish at Indiana University. Author of some seventy books with university and trade presses, he is publishing *ABC of Translation* (Black Widow Press) in March and *Borges at Eighty* (New Directions) in May. Carcanet in England will published his *Selected Poems*.

/Tom BUNSTEAD

Tom Bunstead was one of the British Centre for Literary Translation's 2011-2012 mentees, working with Margaret Jull Costa. His translations include the acclaimed *Polish Boxer* by Eduardo Halfon, which was a collaborative translation with Ollie Brock, Lisa Dillman, Daniel Hahn, and Anne Mclean. "From now on, according to Schopenauer," Tom's translation of an essay by Enrique Vila-Matas, was chosen by documentA to feature in its *Book of Books*, and Tom has translations of novels forthcoming by Premio de Novela Histórica 'Ciudad de Zaragoza' 2012 winner Antonio Garrido and Premio Nadal finalist Nicolás Casariego. Tom's own writing has appeared at >kill author, readysteadybook, the Paris Review Blog, and in the *Independent* and the *TLS*.

Cristina FERNÁNDEZ CUBAS\

Cristina Fernández Cubas was born in Arenys de Mar, Barcelona, in 1945. Since the publication of her first volume of short stories in 1980, she has become an undeniable point of reference for the generations of short story writers to have followed. She is the author of five short story collections, *Mi hermana elba, Los altillos del brumal, El ángulo del horror, Con agatha en estambul*, and *Parientes pobres del diablo*; the novels *El año de gracia* and *El columpio*; a play, *Hermanas de sangre*; and a groundbreaking memoir, *Cosas que ya no existen*, a book warmly received by both the critics and the public, which is known for having shaped one of the most fascinating and unique literary universes of Spanish literature. She has been translated into ten languages. Her complete stories were published recently by Tusquets, paying homage to her literary career, for which she received the Premio Cuidad de Barcelona and the Premio Salambó for the best book published in Spanish in 2008.

/Antonio GAMONEDA

Antonio Gamoneda was born in Oviedo in 1931. His father was a modernist poet whose career was cut short by his early death. The young Antonio reputedly learned to read during the Spanish Civil War, when schools were closed, by immersing himself in his father's poems. His own first book, *Sublevación inmóvil*, published in 1960, was a runner-up for the Adonais Prize. Working with progressive cultural organizations, Gamoneda didn't publish another book of poems until after the fall of Franco. Then, in 1977, he published the impressive long poem *Descripción de la mentira* (León, 1977). After that followed *Lápidas* (Madrid, 1987) and *Edad*, which won the National Prize for Literature in Spain.

In 1992, *Libro del frío* was published. An expanded and revised version included Frío de límites, a collaboration with the artist Antoni Tàpies. *Arden las pérdidas* was published in 2003 and *La luz*, a new collected poetry (1947–2004) was published in 2004. In 2006, Gamoneda was awarded the Reina Sofia Award and the Cervantes Prize, the highest honor in Spanish literature.

Forrest GANDER\

Forrest Gander is a writer and translator with degrees in geology and English literature. His book *Core Samples from the World* was a finalist for the Pulitzer Prize and the National Book Critics Circle Award. His recent translations include *Watchword* by Pura López Colomé and, with Kyoko Yoshida, *Spectacle* & Pigsty by Kiwao Nomura, winner of the Best Translated Book Award in 2012. Forthcoming from Shearsman Editions is Gander's anthology, *Panic Cure: Poetry from Spain for the 21st Century.*

/Pere GIMFERRER

Pere Gimferrer's literary work in Spanish includes the poetry collections *Arde el mar* (1966), which won the National Prize for Poetry, *Amor en vilo* (2006), *Interludio azul* (2006) and *Tornado* (2008). His Catalan work includes the novel *Fortuny* (1983), which won the Ramon Llull and Critica prizes, and *El vendaval* (1988), for which he won the National Poetry Prize for the second time. His life's work has seen him awarded the National Prize for Spanish Literature (1998) and the International Octavio Paz Prize for Poetry and Criticism (2006).

Lucy GREAVES\

Lucy Greaves learned Spanish and discovered her passion for translation at Cambridge University. She then lived and worked in Colombia, Peru, Chile, and Switzerland before going on to earn an MA in Literary Translation at the University of East Anglia. She now works as a freelance translator based in the UK. When not translating, she teaches skiing.

/Daniel HAHN

Daniel Hahn is a writer, editor, and translator. His translations include fiction by José Eduardo Agualusa and José Luís Peixoto, and nonfiction by writers ranging from Portuguese Nobel literature laureate José Saramago to Brazilian footballer Pelé.

Catherine HAMMOND\

Catherine Hammond has a BA in Spanish from the University of Michigan, Ann Arbor, and an MFA from Arizona State University in creative writing. Poems translated from Olvido García Valdés' collection *And We Were All Alive / Y todos estábamos vivos* appear as a chapbook, *House Surrounded by Scaffold*, from Mid-American Review. She also has translations in *American Poetry Review, Field, Hayden's Ferry Review, Drunken Boat,* and many other national magazines. Hammond's own poetry has been anthologized in *Fever Dreams: Contemporary Arizona Poetry* from University of Arizona Press, in *MARGIN: Exploring Modern Magical Realism*, and in *Yellow Silk* from Warner Books. She has three Pushcart nominations.

/Mara Faye LETHEM

Mara Faye Lethem is a Brooklyn-born, Barcelona-based writer and literary translator from Catalan and Spanish. Her translations have appeared in *The Best American Non-Required Reading 2010, Granta,* the *Paris Review* and *McSweeney's.* In Spring 2013, her translation of Patricio Pron's *My Father's Ghost Is Climbing in the Rain* will be published by Knopf in the US and Faber and Faber in the UK. She is currently working on novels by Eduardo Sacheri and Marc Pastor.

Francisco MACÍAS\

Francisco Macías, a Mexican-born American, currently resides in Fredericksburg, Virginia, and works at the Library of Congress in Washington, D.C. He has served the Library as a Senior Legal Information Analyst since 2007. He is a regular blogger for In Custodia Legis, the official blog of the Law Library of Congress. He is also currently the president of the Library of Congress Hispanic Cultural Society and a fellow of the Library of Congress Leadership Development Program. Before joining the Library of Congress, he held an eclectic array of jobs, all of which involved aspects of Spanish philology and pedagogy. Two of his translations have been published: *De cruz y media luna/From Cross and Crescent Moon* by Elvia Ardalani and the *Selected Poems of César Antonio Molina*. He also served as the coordinating editor for a joint project between the Miguel Hernández Foundation and the University of Texas-Pan American Press: a centennial anniversary edition of academic essays commemorating the work of Spanish poet and playwright Miguel Hernández titled *Miguel Hernández desde América* by editors Aitor L. Larrabide and Elvia Ardalani. His forthcoming work includes *The Transfigured Heart* by Dolores Castro and *The Being of the Household Beings* by Elvia Ardalani.

/Berta VIAS MAHOU

Berta Vias Mahou was born in Madrid in 1961, and studied geography and history (specializing in ancient history). A writer and literary translator, she is the author of three novels—*Leo en la cama* (Espasa Narrativa, 1999), *Los pozos de la nieve* (Acantilado, 2008) and *Venían a buscarlo a él* (Acantilado, 2010, winner of the Premio Dulce Chacón de Narrativa 2011)—as well as a book of stories *Ladera norte* (Acantilado, 2001), in which "The Devil Lives in Lisbon" appears; an essay on *La imagen de la mujer en la literatura* (Anaya, 2000), and three young adult novels. She has translated writers including Goethe, Zweig, Schnitzler, Joseph Roth, Gertrud Kolmar, and Ödön von Horváth.

Anne MCLEAN\

Anne McLean translates Latin American and Spanish novels, short stories, memoirs, and other writings by authors including Héctor Abad, Javier Cercas, Julio Cortázar, Evelio Rosero, Juan Gabriel Vásquez, and Enrique Vila-Matas. Her translation of Ignacio Martínez de Pisón's *To Bury the Dead* was published by Parthian Press in 2009.

/Valerie MILES

Valerie Miles is an American writer, translator, and editor living in Barcelona, Spain. She was the editorial director of Emecé Editores and associate director of Alfaguara before launching Duomo ediciones in 2008, where she also oversaw the New York Review of Books classics collection in Spanish. In 2003 she founded *Granta* magazine's Spanish language project together with Aurelio Major and saw the publication of their highly celebrated Best of Young Spanish

Language Novelists issue in 2010. Her articles and stories have been published in *La Vanguardia, ABCD*, and in magazines such as the *Paris Review, Harper's* and *Granta*, among others. She is a professor in the postgraduate program of Literary Translation in the Pompeu i Fabra University and has translated for *Granta*, New Directions, and many other publishers. Recently, she has published a book of conversations with the most important writers in the Spanish language (Javier Marías, Mario Vargas Llosa, Enrique Vila-Matas, Carlos Fuentes, Ana María Matute, Juan Goytisolo, etc.), *Mil bosques en una bellota*, asking each of them what they consider their very best pages of a lifetime of writing. It will be published in English by Open Letter in 2013.

César Antonio MOLINA\

César Antonio Molina (La Coruña, 1952) holds degrees in law and information science. His dissertation, *La prensa literaria española*, was published in three volumes. He was professor of literary theory and criticism at the Complutense University of Madrid and has taught humanities and journalism courses at the Charles III University of Madrid for the past eight years. He was also the coordinator of humanities courses for the summer sessions at the Complutense University of Madrid. From 1985 to 1996 he worked at the newspapers *Cambio 16* and *Diario 16*, where he became deputy director and head of the culture and entertainment sections, as well as the literary and cultural supplements. In 1996 he joined the Círculo de Bellas Artes as managing director. In 2004 he became director of the Instituto Cervantes, and in July 2007 he was appointed Cultural Minister of Spain, a post he held until April 2009. He has published more than thirty books, primarily essays, prose, and poetry. His poetry has appeared in numerous anthologies and has been translated into several languages. In 2005 he published the book of essays *En honor de Hermes*, the poetry collection *En el mar de ánforas*, and the novel *Fuga de amor*. In 2006 he published the poetry anthology *El rumor del tiempo*. He was awarded the medal of the Royal and Distinguished Spanish Order of Charles III. He was named a Chevalier of the Ordre des Arts et des Lettres of the French governement. He was honored by the Italian government with the Cavaliere di Gran Croce de la Orden al Mérito medal and awarded the highest honor of Chile, the O'Higgins Gold Medal, and the Castelao Medal of Galicia. He is currently the director of The International Center for the Research, Development, and Innovation in Reading/Casa de Lector.

/Miquel DE PALOL

Miquel de Palol lives in Barcelona and writes in Catalan. He is the author of fiction, poetry, short stories, and essays. His first novel, *El jardí dels Set Crepuscles*, was awarded the Joan Creixells Prize, the Serra D'Or Critics' Prize, the Catalan and National Critic's Prize for Catalan Literature from the Generalitat de Catalunya, and the Ojo Crítico Prize. He has also won the Ciudad de Barcelona Prize and the Josep Pla Prize for Catalan Narrative.

Ignacio MARTÍNEZ DE PISÓN\

Ignacio Martínez de Pisón was born in Zaragoza in 1960 and has lived in Barcelona since 1982. He has degrees in Spanish and Italian from the Universidad de Zaragoza and the Universitat Central de Barcelona, repectively. His first book was published in 1984. He is the author of several film scripts and more than a dozen books, such as the novels *Carreteras secundarias, El tiempo de las mujeres* (2003), *Dientes de leche* (2008, Giuseppe Acerbi Prize), and *El día de mañana* (2011, Ciutat de Barcelona Prize and Critics' Prize), as well as the nonfiction book *Enterrar a los muertos* (2005, Rodolfo Walsh and Dulce Chacón Prizes).

/Juan Antonio MASOLIVER RÓDENAS

Juan Antonio Masoliver Ródenas (Barcelona, Spain, 1939) was professor of Spanish and Latin American literature at the University of Westminster in London and currently teaches in the Masters of Creative Writing program at the University Pompeu Fabra. He lives in El Masnou (Barcelona). He is a literary critic for the *Cultura/s* supplement of *La Vanguardia* in Barcelona. In Mexico he is or has been contributor to *Vuelta, La Jornada Semanal, Letras Libres,* Fractal and Crítica, among others. A wide range of his articles and essays on Spanish and Mexican literature were collected in *Voces contemporáneas* (Contemporary Voices, 2004) and *Las libertades enlazadas* (2000), respectively. As an author he has published the story collections *La sombra del triángulo* (1996), *La noche de la conspiración de la pólvora* (2006) and most recently *La calle Fontanills* (2010), as well as the novels *Retiro lo escrito* (1988), *Beatriz Miami* (1991) and *La puerta del inglés* (2001). He has translated Cesare Pavese, Giorgio Saviane, Carson McCullers, Djuna Barnes, and Vladimir Nabokov, among others. His poetic works are collected in *Poesía reunida* (Collected Poems, 1999). Subsequently he published *La memoria sin tregua* (2002), *Sònia* (2008) and a book of poems in Catalan, *El laberint del cos* (2008).

Samantha SCHNEE\

Samantha Schnee is a founding editor of at Words Without Borders. She is the former senior editor of *Zoetrope: All-Story*, a literary journal founded by Francis Ford Coppola that won the 2001 National Magazine Award for fiction. She translates from the Spanish.

/Martha TENNENT

Martha Tennent, a translator from Catalan and Spanish, was born in the United States, but has lived most of her life in Barcelona, receiving her B.A. and Ph.D in English from the University of Barcelona. She was the editor of *Training for the New Millennium: Pedagogies for Translation and Interpreting*. She recently translated the novels *Death in Spring* by Mercè Rodoreda, *The Invisible City* by Emili Rosales, and *The Violin of Auschwitz* by Maria Àngels Anglada. Her work has appeared in *Epiphany, Two Lines, Words Without Borders, Public Space, World Literature Today, PEN America*, and *Review of Contemporary Fiction*. Her translation *The Selected Stories of Mercè Rodoreda* received a grant from the National Endowment for the Arts.

Olvido GARCÍA VALDÉS\

Olvido García Valdés (Asturias, España, 1950) resides in Toledo. Her poetry collections, except for her most recent, *Lo solo del animal*, have been published together in one volume, *Esa polilla que delante de mí revolotea (Poesía reunida)*. She has translated Pier Paolo Pasolini's *La religión de mi tiempo y Larga carretera de arena* and contributed to a comprehensive anthology of poetry of Anna Akhmatova and Marina Tsvetaeva in Spanish translation. She also authored the biographical study *Teresa de Jesús* and is co-editor of the magazines *Los Infolios* and *El signo del gorrión*. In 2007 she was awarded the Premio Nacional de Poesía (National Poetry Prize) for her collection *Y todos estábamos vivos*.

/Pedro ZARRALUKI

Pedro Zarraluki (Barcelona, 1954) is the author of two books of short stories, *Galería de enormidades* and *Retrato de familia con catástrofe* (both with Anagrama). As a novelist, he has published: *El responsable de las ranas* (Anagrama, 1990), *La historia del silencio* (Anagrama 1994), *Hotel Astoria* (Anagrama, 1997) and *Para amantes y ladrones* (Anagrama, 2000). His novel *Un encargo difícil* (Destino, 2005) was granted the Nadal Award and was shortlisted for the José Manuel Lara Foundation Award. Following the compilation of stories *Humor pródigo* (Destino, 2007), he published the novel *Todo eso que tanto nos gusta* (Destino, 2008). In March 2012 he will publish his first novel for young readers, *El hijo del virrey* (Siruela, 2012). *La historia del silencio* will be published in English translation next year by Hispabooks.

Juan Eduardo ZÚÑIGA\

Juan Eduardo Zúñiga was born in Madrid and in college studied philosophy and fine art, specializing in Slavic languages. His first book, *Inútiles totales*, came out in 1951, the next, *El coral y las aguas*, in 1962, and *Artículos sociales de Mariano José de Larra* in 1976. A proponent of the novel as a tool for memory, Zúñiga set his collection of stories *Largo noviembre de Madrid* (1980) in and around the Spanish Civil War and its aftermath, and these themes have recurred throughout his later work: *La tierra será un paraíso* (1989), *Misterios de las noches y los días* (1992), *Flores de plomo* (Ramón Gómez de la Serna prize-winner, 1999) and *Capital de la gloria* (2003), which won Spain's Nacional de la Crítica Prize and the prestigious Salambó. His most recent collection of stories is *Brillan monedas oxidadas* (Galaxia Gutenberg, 2010). His knowledge of Russian and Bulgarian culture—in 1990 he published *Sofía*, an essay on the Bulgarian capital—prompted him to look deeper into celebrated writers from Eastern Europe. *Desde los bosques nevados* (Galaxia Gutenberg), a study of Pushkin, Turgenev, and Chekhov, came out in 2010 and won the International Terenci Moix Prize.

Editors

\

/Javier APARICIO

Javier Aparicio Maydeu (1964) holds a PhD in Spanish philology. He is professor of Spanish literature and comparative literature at the Universitat Pompeu Fabra in Barcelona and associate dean of the faculty of humanities and head of the masters program in publishing at IDEC-Universitat Pompeu Fabra. He is a literary critic for *El País*. His publications include two volumes of criticism of contemporary world fiction: *Lecturas de ficción contemporánea. De Kafka a Ishiguro* (Cátedra, 2008) and *El desguace de la tradición. En el taller de la narrativa del siglo XX* (Cátedra, 2011).

Aurelio MAJOR\

Aurelio Major (1963) is a poet, translator, and editor. He was editorial director of Octavio Paz's Editorial Vuelta, and of Tusquets Editores, among other publishers in Mexico and Barcelona, and is currently editorial consultant for several European publishing groups. He has edited in Spanish the works of Basil Bunting and George Oppen, and is translator of the work of Eliot Weinberger and Susan Sontag. His edition, with an introduction, of Edmund Wilson's *Selected Critical Writings* was published in 2008. He is co-founding editor, with Valerie Miles, of the Spanish edition of *Granta* magazine.

/Mercedes MONMANY

Mercedes Monmany (Barcelona, 1957) is the author of *Una infancia de escritor* (Xordica, 1997), *Don Quijote en los Cárpatos* (Huerga and Fierro, 2009) and *Vidas de mujer* (Alliance, 1999). She has translated work by Francis Ponge, Attilio Bertolucci, and Philippe Jaccottet, and edited volumes by authors including Alvaro Mutis, Margaret Atwood, Bánffy Miklós, and Gesualdo Bufalino. She edits the literary essay series La Rama Dorada published by Huerga and Fierro. One of the most important literary critics in Spain, she contributes to numerous publications and writes a weekly column for the cultural supplement of the newspaper *ABC*.

Copyright Acknowledgments

About
Words without Borders

Words without Borders is a ten-year-old nonprofit organization dedicated to the promotion of cultural understanding through the translation, publication, and promotion of the finest contemporary international literature. Every month at wordswithoutborders.org we publish ten to twelve new works by international writers. Our archive of over 1,600 pieces from 119 countries includes work by Adonis, Can Xue, Ko Un, J. M. G. Le Clézio, Stanisław Lem, Saadat Hasan Manto, Herta Müller, Boualem Sansal, and Tomas Tranströmer, as well as hundreds of emerging talents. In addition we have partnered with publishing houses to release five print anthologies, the most recent of which is *Tablet & Pen: Literary Landscapes of the Modern Middle East*. Words without Borders is currently developing an education program that will provide tools and resources to help high school and college educators incorporate contemporary international literature into their classes.

About
SPAIN arts & culture

Established in 1999, the Spain-USA Foundation is a nonprofit organization dedicated to promoting, supporting and developing Spanish cultural and educational activities in the United States. Together with the Embassy of Spain in Washington D.C., the Foundation organizes the SPAIN arts & culture program featuring exhibitions, conferences, showcases, and performances throughout each year to highlight the work of both internationally renowned as well as less widely discovered Spanish artists in fields such as design, urban culture, architecture, visual arts, film, performing arts, literature and music. Through the SPAIN arts & culture program, the Spain-USA Foundation brings a taste of the creativity, rich history, and incredible talent of Spanish artists to the American public.